Deadly Duty

"Shad Corey murdered Holt Ricket. I'm going after him."

Rita gripped Sarboe's arms. "You're not fooling me, Ben. You're going after Corey because you're in love with Linda and you don't want him to have her. If you ever loved me, you'll stay here where you're needed."

Sarboe pulled away from her and stepped into the saddle. "Remember it was your idea for me to pack this star. It comes first. It has to come first to any man who pins it on if he's worth a damn."

He reined around and presently he was lost to sight in the pines. Within the hour he found a woman's handkerchief in the road. It was no accident, he thought. It would strike Corey's perverted sense of drama to lure him here and dry gulch him. Then he saw two horses ahead. Sarboe swung his horse back; he dug in the steel and headed directly for the ridge. He heard Linda scream as Corey's gun thundered, the slug falling short. The second bullet snapped by within a foot of his head.

BY GUN AND SPUR

BY GUN AND SPUR

Wayne D. Overholser

PaperJacks LTD.

TORONTO   NEW YORK

PaperJacks

BY GUN AND SPUR

PaperJacks LTD

330 STEELCASE RD. E., MARKHAM, ONT. L3R 2M1
210 FIFTH AVE., NEW YORK, N.Y. 10010

PaperJacks edition published December 1987

This is a work of fiction in its entirety. Any resemblance to actual people, places or events is purely coincidental.

CDN ISBN 0-7701-0831-8
US ISBN 0-7701-0559-9

BY GUN AND SPUR

INTRODUCTION

If you take U.S. Highway 20 west from Burns, you will cross the high Oregon desert. You will go through Hampton, Brothers, and Millican, made famous by Billy Rahn as the "One man town"; tiny places in a nearly empty land. Unless you have been told, you would not dream that once here on the desert there were homesteaders' shacks, the homes of men who plowed up the sage and planted grain and paid five dollars a barrel for water. No, you would not dream that, for they have gone and the desert has claimed its own.

You will keep driving westward with the Cascades gradually growing nearer, you will cross irrigation ditches, you will swing past the foot of Pilot Butte and you will find yourself in town. Perhaps you have planned to stay the night here, for there are good motels and it has been a long way across the desert.

Your first impression will be startling. Here is a town with a striking personality entirely its own. You will see junipers and pines and sagebrush in the most unlikely places, you will find lava rock jutting up in back yards and front yards, you will see the Deschutes River flowing through town and you will see Mirror Pond, and it may be that you will bring a loaf of bread and feed the ducks and geese and swans.

If you tarry, you will think that this would be a good town in which to live. You will find churches, schools, a hospital; you will drink the best water in the world, and you will find yourself looking at scenery that will hold its own against any kind of competition. If you're a mountain climber, a hunter, a fisherman, well, here is your country. After fifty years of settlement, the wilderness is still only a stone's throw away. But most of all, you'll like the people, for here is a country which cherishes its heritage of the old West.

Swift River is not the name of this town, and this is not the history of it. If you have time and inclination to

*read its history, you will find no mention of Ben Sarboe
and Rita Gentry and Fred Purvane, but you will find the
names of others who had their courage and faith, and,
like them, the kind of vision that took them beyond the
horizon.*

*If you stay awhile, you may meet some of these people
who have watched a dream come true and have helped
with their hands and their hearts. If you ask them they'll
tell you about the first irrigation projects, the struggle
of the titans when two railroads were built up the
Deschutes, the coming of the two big mills. But they
won't stop there. They'll point to the years ahead, for
this is a young town filled with the vigor of youth. There
are many more dreams to be made come true.*

*This is a story of how a town was born, no more and
no less. It is not history, but it might have happened this
way.*

Chapter I

PORTENT OF PROGRESS

IT WAS A land of old, long-gone violence reaching back
to an age when the earth had rumbled and trembled and
rolled out streams of molten lava that lay now, centuries
later, in broken and twisted piles, desert patches in a pine
wilderness. On one side there were sky-reaching peaks
whose glaciers gave birth to icy streams that roared down
from the high country; on the other there was the gray-
toned desert of sage and rabbit brush and bunchgrass,
dotted by wind-shaped junipers. Too, it was an empty
land, silent except for a coyote call or the quack of ducks
southbound in fall, a land where a man could hear the

wind-song in the pines. It was a land that suited Ben Sarboe.

The Silver Lake stage came wheeling through the pines as Sarboe, content with his morning catch, left the Deschutes and walked across a meadow to his cabin. He leaned against the log wall and dropped his half dozen foot-long trout in the grass. Turning, he raised his hand in greeting as the stage stopped.

"How's things, Barney?" Sarboe asked.

"Damned cold for April." Barney Johns wiped a hand across his leathery face. "Have to feel once in a while to see if it's still there. One of these days I'm going to Arizona."

"I've been there," Sarboe said. "You'll come back."

Johns tossed a mail sack at Sarboe's feet. "I doubt if I will, son. What gets me is that you've been everywhere and seen everything and you still ain't got sense enough to get out of this damned cold country."

"I quit looking for Heaven," Sarboe said. "I'm satisfied."

Johns snorted. "Looks to me like you could have got a little nearer Heaven before you quit looking. Well, time to roll. So long."

"So long."

Sarboe watched the coach wheel away, splashing through mud puddles left by slowly melting snow patches at the edge of the road. It was well into April, but it had only been the last few days that winter had reluctantly begun its retreat from the Deschutes country. Just two seasons here, the old-timers said cynically, winter and August. It was a statement which came close to the truth, as Sarboe had already learned.

He picked up his trout and went inside. Because his cabin was on the stage road, it had been selected as a post office for the few scattered ranchers who lived closer to Sarboe's place than Prineville, the only town in Central Oregon. There was little pay and a good deal of responsibility, but Sarboe had not objected to giving this small service. It brought people to his door, often to visit and sometimes to eat with him, breaks in the monotony of living that would otherwise have been intolerable.

Laying the trout on the table, Sarboe dumped the mail and sorted it, slipping envelopes and packages into the rack he had hung near the door. He reached the last letter and stopped, shocked by surprise. It was addressed to him.

For a long moment he stood motionless, staring at the envelope. He had kept no links with the past. Not that he was ashamed of anything he had done. Rather it was a case of letting the old turbulence die, of holding tenaciously to the peace which he had found in the wilderness.

Sarboe dropped the letter on the table, thinking of the countless smoky miles that lay behind him, of the dozens of places where he had lingered. Sooner or later he had always gone on, for until he had come to the Deschutes he had never found a place he liked. He had found it now.

He thought of his neighbors, trying to scrape a living out of a wilderness with a handful of cows. They were good people, honest people, the kind who took anything life gave them and hung on. They had accepted him at once. All but the Rickets who were a law unto themselves, old Cap and his boys, Verd and Holt. Sarboe did not pretend to understand the Rickets. He saw them occasionally when they came for the mail; they took it without a thank you or by your leave, and rode away at once, dark unfriendly men.

Sarboe built a fire, spooned grease into a pan, and dropped two trout into it. Then he returned to the table and, picking up the envelope, studied the big-lettered writing. There were places in California and Arizona where the name Ben Sarboe meant a great deal. Now he vaguely wished he had changed his name when he had settled here. Someone had found out where he lived and wanted him to come back and pin a star on again. Well, he wouldn't do it.

He tore the envelope open, took out the letter, and glanced at the name on the bottom of the sheet. Mike Kelly! Relief ran through him. He should have known. Kelly had spent most of the previous summer with him, riding through the junipers and sage to the north and east, and talking every evening about the bright future that this country held. Sarboe had mentally pegged the talk ninety-nine per cent wind. Now, reading the letter, he changed his mind.

> The Dalles, Oregon
> April 2, 1903

Dear Ben:

I hope you have survived your rugged Central Oregon winter and have come out of hibernation. If you haven't, you will, pronto, because progress is moving in. As I said last summer, there is no reason why ten thousand people can't live in the Deschutes country and make a good living. All it needs is someone with foresight and gumption enough to get water on the land, and nobody ever accused Ma Kelly's boy of not having foresight and gumption. The Lord didn't put a tongue in my head for nothing. All I needed was the dollars.

Well, Ben, I spent half the winter working on George Dallam, and I finally made him see the light. He's backing me, and he's got the dollars. I've secured a segregation of twenty thousand acres under the Carey Land Act, so in less than a month I'll be ready. The minute I get men and teams started on a ditch, the settlers will flock in. Take my word for that.

I know you won't like this, but remember that if it isn't me, it will be someone else. With population growing and the big cities consuming more and more food, we cannot afford to overlook good land such as that which lies along the Deschutes. We'll both make some money, but we'll also be doing our country a patriotic service.

Now I'm asking one small favor. I'm making arrangements for hay to be hauled from Crooked River, but I'll need something besides salt side for my men. I'd like for you to round up fifty head of steers and have them on hand by May first. We'll butcher as we need them. I'll see that you are properly reimbursed, and there will be a little extra for your trouble.

Your friend,
Mike

P.S. Say, I met a friend of yours in The Dalles who is a pefect example of blonde pulchritude. You sure missed a bet with her, boy. She thinks you're something pretty damn special, and from what she says, you made a name for yourself in Colorado. You shouldn't hide your light under a basket, Ben. Mike Kelly never does. How would you like to pack a star in my new town?

Mike

Sarboe crumpled the letter and threw it across the room. It was like Mike, breezy and interesting, braggy and complimentary. Sarboe wondered briefly who the perfect example of blonde pulchritude was. He moved to the stove and turned the trout over, his mind swinging to more disturbing parts of the letter. *Progress is moving in. I know you won't like this. We'll both make money. Settlers will flock in.*

For a time anger gripped him. He had seen progress move into a wilderness; he knew what it did. The Lord made the world one way and man did his damnedest to change it, usually for the worst. Well, Mike Kelly would bring him out of hibernation all right. It would serve Kelly right if he gave him something in return, something like a good punch on the nose.

He ate, the anger dying. There was a good deal of truth in what Kelly said about population growing and cities demanding more and more food. Too, there was need for free land. The day when Uncle Sam could give a man a farm had been gone for a generation. That is, a good farm ready for the plow. The answer was here in the deep lava soil. Kelly was right, too, in saying that someone else would open this country for settlement if he didn't.

Sarboe saddled his roan gelding, thinking that Cap Ricket was the only cowman he could call a neighbor who would have fifty steers to sell. There was no hurry, but Sarboe was not one to sit around when a chore waited to be done. He couldn't hold back what Kelly called progress, so he might as well go along. If Ricket wouldn't let him have the steers, he'd swing north to Crooked River where he would have no trouble getting as many as Kelly could use.

He was in the saddle when he thought of the mail. He might as well save the Rickets the trouble of coming after it. Stepping down, he took the mail from the Ricket pigeonhole and dropped it into a sack. Then he saw the trout he had left from dinner, and after a moment's hesitation, picked them up and slipped them into the sack with the mail.

Riding directly east, Sarboe was out of the pines within half an hour and among the junipers, thinly scattered in the sage. He climbed through open country that lifted steadily to the crest of a range of hills paralleling the river, the wind cutting into him with bone-deep penetration. Except for a ragged row of creamy clouds hiding the high peaks to the west, the sky was a sweeping blue vault. Still, the sun was without warmth, and he pulled the collar of his sheepskin up around his neck, for here there was nothing to temper the chill thrust of the wind.

It was midafternoon when he topped the ridge and came down to the Rickets' Circle R. He had never been here before, so he rode in slowly, looking the place over and thinking it was as coldly unfriendly as the Rickets themselves. The house was built of lava rock, a sprawling two-story structure that was, as far as Sarboe knew, the biggest house on the high desert. It glared at Sarboe, grim and austere, the kind of house a man might build if he expected some day to defend himself against armed assault.

For the first time since he had come to Central Oregon, Sarboe wished he had his gun. It had been a relief to hang it up, for he had spent the eight years before coming here with his gun as a constant companion. Lawman, shotgun guard, trouble shooter of one kind or another, Ben Sarboe had passed from job to job in mining camps and border towns with powder smoke a constant stench in his nostrils.

Now, staring at Cap Ricket's big house, Sarboe thought one reason he liked it on the Deschutes was that here for the first time since he was a boy he could relax his vigilance, he could sleep soundly, he could ride away and leave his front door unlocked and be reasonably sure that nothing would be bothered.

It was the way of life in this country, a land where neighbors lived ten miles apart. Because of distance, they seldom saw each other, and were properly appreciative of the few contacts they had. Again Sarboe had to make a mental exception of the Rickets who seemed content to be let alone.

There was no sign of life about the ranch except for the faint trace of smoke from the chimney. Sarboe had to look closely to see it, for the wind caught the smoke and whipped it into oblivion the instant it appeared. He dismounted and tied in front of the house, gaze moving from the pole corrals to the log barn and sheds. There were no cows, no chickens, no hogs. Not even a horse in sight. No garden of flowers, no grass in the shifting sandy soil around the house.

Sarboe untied his sack from the saddle, thinking that this was the craziest place that a man could find to build a house. The nearest trees were a few wind-bent junipers fifty yards to the south. Just the rocky slope rising to the west, a gray desert to the east flung out for miles, rimrock and valley, land and sky. There was, Sarboe conceded, a grim sort of beauty about it, but he doubted that Cap Ricket or his sons had ever considered anything as intangible as beauty.

No one was here, or there would be a horse in the corral. Still, Sarboe had seen the smoke, so they had not been gone long, and it was possible they might be back soon. He turned toward the house, knocked on the front door just to be sure, and went around to the back. Again a tap on the door brought no answer. He started to turn away, then remembered the sack that was in his hand.

Sarboe tried the knob. It turned and he pushed the door open. Warm air rushed at him. He crossed the kitchen to the big table, dropping his sack on it, and went out quickly, a vague uneasiness in him. No one else on the high desert would object to what he had done, but the Rickets would not be judged by what others would do or think.

Sarboe closed the door and went back to his horse. He waited there for a time, uncertainty tugging at him. If the Rickets were gone for the day, he'd be ahead to ride on to Crooked River. He smoked a cigarette, the sun moving westward, and then he saw them coming from the south, Cap riding between his two sons.

Apparently they saw him at the same time he saw them, for they immediately brought their horses to a faster pace. Cap was one of the tallest men Sarboe had ever seen. He must have been close to sixty, but in spite of his age, he rode straight up in the saddle, a rigid erectness that was typical of him whether he was on foot or forking a horse.

He wore his black hair long, his beard was wiry and fell far down on his chest, and neither hair nor beard showed the slightest trace of gray.

They reined up twenty feet from Sarboe, Cap's great voice booming out, "What are doing here, Sarboe?"

For a moment Sarboe gave no answer. He felt the pressure of their hostility, and anger rose in him. They were aliens in an otherwise friendly land, and they never seemed more unnatural to it than they did now.

Sarboe's gaze touched Verd's ugly scarred face. He was a squat thick-bodied man with a wide jaw and black eyes that were fixed on Sarboe in an unwavering stare. Sarboe swung his gaze to Holt, the younger son who was built like his father, tall and slender and long-boned. There the resemblance ended, for a while Cap gave an impression of grim, rock-lick honesty, Holt was never able to quite meet another man's eyes. His face was thin, and a long, hawk-like nose added to the impression of thinness.

"Came over on business," Sarboe said. "I want to buy some steers if you've got any you want to let go."

"Going into the cattle business?" Cap asked skeptically.

"Sort of. I want fifty head, delivered the first of May."

"He's lying," Verd said. "He just wants to snoop."

"You're enough to make a man snoop," Sarboe said irritably. "You act like you're hiding something."

"Our business." Cap leaned forward, hands gripping the saddle horn. "But we ain't. Savvy?"

Sarboe shrugged. "Sure. I brought your mail. Likewise some trout I caught this morning."

"We don't want your damned fish," Verd burst out, "and we're able to ride after our own mail."

"Shut up," Cap said testily. "He's just trying to be neighborly, which same is something a chuckle-head like you wouldn't understand. Where'd you leave the mail and fish, Sarboe?"

"On the kitchen table. Couldn't raise nobody when I knocked . . ."

"Just walked in and made yourself at home, now didn't you?" Verd asked. "Looks like you need to be taught some manners, friend."

Verd swung out of the saddle. Sarboe was a chunky, medium-tall man, his shoulders and arms hard-muscled, but beside Verd he seemed very slight. He stood his ground, watching Verd move toward him like a plodding stud horse, and he knew he had no chance if he came to grips with the man. He had heard of his barroom fights in Prineville. The stories were not pretty.

Casually Sarboe turned to Cap. He said, "About them steers . . ." Then Verd was a step away and Sarboe wheeled. Moving with the same speed that had made him a successful gunfighter, Sarboe drove his right fist to Verd's jaw, the blow hitting the man with the brutal force of an upswinging axhandle. Verd sprawled flat on his back and lay there for a moment, half-stunned.

Holt cried out, an involuntary sound jolted out of him by surprise. Cap wheeled his horse between Sarboe and Verd who was getting to his feet, his movements slow as if he were uncertain whether he'd remain upright.

"Serves you right," Cap said in disgust. "When you try to teach a man manners, you'd better be damned sure you can do the job." He looked at Sarboe, sudden humor in his black eyes. "You pack quite a wallop, friend. Didn't figure you had it in you. Now what was it you wanted them steers for?"

Completely angry, Sarboe said, "To hell with you. I'll be riding."

"I ain't one to apologize to nobody," Cap pressed, eager now, "but Verd is a mite hasty. We just ain't used to having folks around."

Sarboe moved to his horse and stepped up. Verd had mounted. He glared at Sarboe, saying nothing. Suddenly Holt laughed, a strange hysterical sound.

"He just likes to fight," Holt said, his voice carrying the same strange note of hysteria. "Fighting's like whiskey is to some men. He'll try you again one of these days."

Ignoring him, Sarboe said, "I just had a letter from Mike Kelly. He stayed with me last summer. Remember him?" Cap nodded, and Sarboe went on, "He's putting in an irrigation system. Wants the beef to feed his men."

For no reason that was evident to Sarboe, Holt began to tremble, his face very pale. Verd cursed sourly. Cap put on a hand to his forehead. He looked like a man who was suddenly afraid, although he had always given the impression of one who did not know fear.

"No deal," Cap said dully. "I'll have no part in bringing a lot of people here. We like this country the way it is."

"We can't stop 'em," Sarboe said, and rode away toward Prineville.

Chapter II

BLONDE GIRL

THAT NIGHT Sarboe camped on Bear Creek. He went on to Crooked River the next day and made arrangements to buy fifty head of steers, delivery date May first. They would not be in good condition, for it had been a slow spring, even on Crooked River which was usually weeks ahead of the piney foothills of the Cascades, but they would have to do.

He stayed one night in Prineville, finding more pleasure in a few drinks, some poker, and the good talk that flowed along the bar than he had expected. He had missed these things. Too, it was a relief to talk to friendly men, their easy words and manners removing the sourness that his meeting with the Rickets had left in his mind.

Sarboe rode home slowly, for there was no urgency in his life these days. There were pleasant things to think about, particularly Kelly's coming, for the big redheaded Irishman had a natural charm that Sarboe had found in few men. But the pleasant thoughts eventually gave way in his mind to the Rickets.

When Sarboe had mentioned the Rickets in Prineville, the responses had run the same. As the barman in the Belle Union had put it, "If the Rickets want to be let alone, they damn well will be. And if that Verd never shows up here, it'll be all right with me. He's like a bad Injun. He never forgets nothing."

It was the sort of warning Sarboe could not discount. He understood Verd, for he had met many like him in the mining camps and border towns where he had carried the star. The ordinary standards by which the average man lived did not apply. As Holt had said, "Fighting's like whiskey is to some men." Trouble would lure Verd Ricket as surely as a magnet draws steel. Sarboe's brief encounter with him had settled nothing. If they both stayed in the country, Verd would try again just as Holt had told Sarboe.

It was Cap and Holt who puzzled Sarboe, Cap who seemed to possess a great courage and a great pride and yet had suddenly been afraid when Sarboe had mentioned Kelly's irrigation project, and Holt, thin-faced and sensitive who had been brought close to hysteria by the fight between Sarboe and Verd.

Apparently Cap had had some money when he had brought his boys to the high desert a few years ago. It had been before Sarboe's time in this country, but he had heard the talk, of how they had driven in a herd of cattle and built a big stone house which everybody else on the desert considered a piece of foolishness. But Sarboe could understand that. Some men liked to make a show, and a big house might be Cap's way of doing it. The thing which puzzled Sarboe was the Rickets' desire to live alone in a country where everybody else placed a high value upon the few human contacts which came their way.

Because Sarboe could find no explanation of the Rickets' way of life, he put them out of his mind. It was evening when he reached the first pines, outposts of a great forest, scattered among the scraggly junipers. For hours he had been riding toward a bowl-like hill known as Pilot Butte, so named because it had long been a landmark to thirsty westbound travelers, promising them that a short distance to the west they would find in the Deschutes an unlimited supply of pure, cold water.

Sarboe angled south of the butte toward the river until he reached the stage road. There the pines were all around him, the gray desert behind. Ahead, miles beyond the desert and rising above the foothills, were the great peaks of the Cascades: Bachelor, Broken Top, the Three Sisters, and Mt. Jefferson. If he lived here a million years, he would never tire of looking at them.

The sun dropped behind the Three Sisters and scarlet banners were flung out across the sky, touching fire to the clouds that hung there. Then the color faded, purple dusk moved in around Sarboe, and the peaks darkened until they were black mounds bulking against the lighter sky.

Sarboe followed the road, the silence complete except for the soft thud of hoofs in pine needles, the faint breath of the wind in the treetops above him, and the liquid whisper of the river to his right. He had often ridden home at this time of day with the night pressing in. He always held his roan down to a slow walk, for there would be nothing to do when he got home but take care of his horses, light a lantern and chop an armful of wood, build a fire, and cook supper.

These past months had formed a definite, unhurried pattern of life for Ben Sarboe, a pattern that had few variations. He would bring two buckets of water from the river, heat a pan of it, and wash dishes. He would read for a while, something he had never had time or desire to do before, and then step outside. If it was a clear night, he might spend an hour staring at the stars, their crystal light washing down upon a forested earth.

He had tried to imagine how it had been centuries before when torment had seized this land, causing it to spew out ribbons of molten rock. Those same stars had been in the sky, the same river flowing like chill silver beside the sullen, cooling piles of lava, the same peaks rearing up against the black sky.

Peace had returned to be marred by transient bands of Snakes or Modocs here for obsidian from which they would shape their arrowheads, or by passage of some solitary mountain man searching for beaver pelts. Then the great silence had settled back.

Discontent gripped Ben Sarboe as he came to the meadow that held his cabin. On this thing he could agree with Cap Ricket and his boys. Cap had said, "We like this country the way it is." It wouldn't remain that way for long. Within a matter of days the peace that is always a part of an empty land would be gone.

Mike Kelly would bring men and teams and scrapers and tons of powder. They'd blast and shovel and fill the air with angry oaths; there would be gunfire and death, for wherever there were men, there would be the product of their frailties: greed and hate and lust. Some good things would come of it as Kelly had promised, but there would be other things that were not good, scars upon a land that had been wild and primitive and beautiful.

Then Sarboe saw the light in his cabin and the flow of his thoughts ran dry. He was angry, for he supposed it was Kelly who had come on sooner than he had indicated. Perhaps his men and horses were camped somewhere between here and Shaniko, the sprawling shipping point that marked the end of steel to the north.

Sarboe dismounted, wondering if he could be civil to Kelly. He needed a month to get used to the idea, and Kelly had robbed him of that month. The door swung open and lamplight lay in a long yellow pool on the grass, but it wasn't Mike Kelly who stood in the doorway. It was a woman, tall, statuesque, her voice inviting when she said, "Come in, Ben."

For a moment Sarboe did not move. He stood in the light, staring at the woman. The lamp was behind her, so he could not see her face, but he sensed something familiar about her. For a moment he mentally groped into his past to identify her. He remembered the postscript to Kelly's letter about the blonde, but that, even if it was the same woman, did not identify his visitor.

She laughed. It was a pleasant sound, not at all jarring like the laughter of so many women Sarboe had known who blatantly placed a dollar value upon their virtue, nor was it the weary laugh of ranchers' wives who could find little pleasure in a hard existence that robbed them of their beauty and their hopes before they were thirty.

"I know," the woman said. "You're thinking I've got a lot of gall moving into your home as if it was mine, but I rode in a couple of hours ago and I couldn't find you, so I helped myself."

"Sure, that was right," he said, and went in.

She moved back into the room and held out her hand to him, manlike in her directness, and the light was upon her face. Then he recognized her, his mind swinging back to his months in Cripple Creek, and for a moment he stood motionless, shocked by surprise. It was Rita Gentry, filled out, a mature and attractive woman. She had been a string-bodied girl the last time he had seen her, but there was nothing stringy about her now.

"Rita!" He took her hand and repeated her name. "Rita! Why, this is as surprising as being visited by an angel."

She laughed. "But it's not the same. I don't want any man mistaking me for an angel. The fact is I'm a devil."

Her hair was amber gold, almost red with the lamplight upon it. Her eyes, he saw, were exactly as they had been when he had known her, so blue they were startling. There was an eagerness about them that indicated she expected life to be exciting, or if it was not, she would make it so. Her lips were full and very red against her naturally light skin, and even when she was quite grave, a smile seemed to be waiting in the corners of her mouth.

"I can't believe you're a devil," he said, "although I have heard that old Satan takes on some mighty pretty disguises."

"Well, just so you understand I'm a schemer. I don't want to take advantage of a trusting man. Now go put your horse away. I'll get supper."

He obeyed, feeling the surge of excitement in him. He had never been a man to let himself be disturbed by women, at least after he had left Cripple Creek. Rita had been disturbance enough, and now she had come back into his life.

He offsaddled, rubbed the horse down, and spilled oats into the manger, noting that the stall beyond his pack animal was occupied by a bay mare that had been ridden hard. He returned to his cabin, thinking of Cal Gentry, an old cowman who had been attracted to Cripple Creek shortly after the strike had been made and had sunk every nickel he owned into the Lucky Lady mine. He'd hit it rich and hired Sarboe to guard the ore shipments, some of it high grade, and before Sarboe had moved to another job, Gentry had been well on the road to becoming a millionaire.

Sarboe had been in love with Rita then and he had never really changed. At least she had been in his thoughts so much he had never had room for another woman. He remembered she had been something of a devil in those days. At seventeen she had been filled with a reckless spirit that drove her out of the house when lightning fried the sky, made her insist on riding horses that were too wild for a woman, and once when Gentry and Sarboe had anticipated an attempt at robbery, she had unexpectedly appeared out of the aspens and brought her horse in alongside Sarboe's. There was a six-gun in her holster and a Winchester held across her saddle horn. Afterwards her father had scolded her soundly and then admitted that her presence might have been responsible for the attack's not coming off.

Rita was frying bacon when Sarboe came in. There was a pot of beans on the stove, biscuits in the oven, and strong coffee the way Sarboe liked it. He sat down, asking, "How's Cal?"

She filled his plate and brought it to him, her face grave. "He died five years ago, Ben. Funny what gold does to some people. Dad set out to drink himself to death and he succeeded. Just too much money too fast."

"I'm sorry," Sarboe said, feeling the inadequacy of anything he could say.

Of all the men he had worked for, Sarboe remembered Cal Gentry best. Rough, intemperate, hard-driving, Gentry had been basically honest. Sarboe had been young then, and a little reckless, and more than once Gentry had talked to him like a father, pointing out that a boom camp had a thousand ways by which a man could go to hell, and Sarboe was trying them all.

"Don't pay no attention to the way I live," Gentry had said. "I'm old. If I can leave something for Rita and still enjoy the days I've got left, I'll be satisfied when I go over the range, but you're young and you're smart enough to profit by my mistakes. Just remember one thing. You're not going to pull anything out of this life unless you put something in. That's my trouble. I never deposited anything."

And Sarboe had profited by Gentry's mistakes. There was never any sure way to know what went into the making of a man, but it had always been Sarboe's feeling that Cal Gentry, more than anyone else, had shaped his life. At least Gentry had made him think and choose so that now Ben Sarboe was very little like the belligerent twenty-one-year-old kid who had once lived in Cripple Creek.

Rita poured a cup of coffee for herself and sat down across the table from Sarboe. She said, "You don't look much different than you used to, Ben. A little heavier and a few lines around your eyes." She looked directly at him. "I never met a man with gray eyes like yours I couldn't trust. Dad liked you a lot. He was pretty unhappy when you drew your time, but he said he knew how it was when you were young. There were a lot of hills and you had to see on the other side of all of them."

"Yeah, I guess it was that way," he admitted. "Well, I've seen over enough hills now. I'm satisfied just to go fishing."

"It's a beautiful country," she said. "I've been here several times, just looking, and I've always thought it would be a wonderful place to live." She looked down at her cup of coffee. "My trouble is that I like people too well to live by myself."

"I haven't been alone. People come by for their mail." He grinned. "That's the only duty I have. Otherwise, it's been a vacation that's lasted a year."

She leaned forward, very serious, "Ben, aren't you tired of . . . just fishing?"

"Not yet."

"I hoped you would be. You see, after Dad died, I sold the mine and traveled, thinking I'd meet up with you. I was terribly in love with you." She laughed. "But I got over that."

"Too bad."

"Oh, I'm not so sure about that. I crossed your trail a dozen times. You had a pair of fiddle feet if a man ever did. Anyhow, I discovered that if I did catch up with you, I couldn't hold you. That's when I began investing my money. Townsites mostly. You know, Ben, I'm either smart or lucky. Every investment I made turned out good."

"Businesswoman," he said.

"Don't hooraw me," she said crossly. "You're not in a position to."

"Oh, I don't know." He leaned back and rolled a smoke. "I'm a good postmaster." He sealed his smoke and raised his eyes to hers. "And a damned fine hermit."

She laughed. "Old man of the mountains." Then the laughter died. "I know how it is with you, Ben. You just got tired of saving other people's money and taking all the risks. All right. You had a vacation coming. Now it's over."

"How do you figure that?"

"I talked to Mike Kelly."

He fished a match out of his vest pocket, staring at her in surprise. "You must be the perfect example of blonde pulchritude. I had a letter from him the other day."

"Did he say that about me?"

Sarboe nodded. "You impressed him."

"I didn't intend to," she said tartly. "I don't like braggy men, and I don't like one who thinks he just has to look at a woman to make her fall in love with him."

Sarboe fired his cigarette. "Sounds as if you don't like Kelly."

"I don't. That's one reason I'm here. The other is that he mentioned you. I didn't even know you were in Oregon until I said something about Colorado and he asked me if I knew you. You must have said you'd been in Cripple Creek."

"Yeah, reckon I did."

She rose. "Well, I'll wash the dishes. That's one way a woman can make herself handy." She picked up a bucket and handed it to him. "But toting water is man's work. Service, Mr. Sarboe."

"Yes ma'am," he said, and taking the bucket, went outside.

Funny the things a man remembered. He walked across the meadow, thinking of his last day in Cripple Creek. He'd drawn his time, saddled up, and ridden out of camp. He hadn't told Rita good-bye and now he had a feeling she had not forgotten. A man had to do so much drifting, Cal Gentry had said. Then he'd said something else that Sarboe had thought about many times. *Do your drifting before you let a woman get her loop on you.*

Sarboe stooped and filled his bucket, memories flooding back into his mind, memories he had forgotten and wanted to forget. He had never been a man to break himself on the whirling stone of goals impossible to attain. Rita had been exactly that, for Gentry had sensed how Sarboe had felt. He had been brutally frank in saying it wouldn't do. Not when Rita was seventeen and Sarboe twenty-one, with Rita just beginning to explore her talents as a woman and Sarboe uncertain of himself and having a hundred hills to ride up so he could see on the other side. Well, everything was different now.

He walked back to the cabin, thinking it was strange that Rita had frankly said she had been in love with him and had tried to find him. He wondered if she knew why he had left Cripple Creek.

Sarboe went in and poured water into a dishpan, glancing obliquely at Rita. She was wearing a soft blue bombazine dress that went well with her light coloring, a dress that was cut to show off her roundness of breasts and hips. She flashed him a smile and busied herself filling the firebox and stacking dishes. He walked back across the room, pulled a chair from the wall, and sat down.

For eight years he had done everything he could to forget Rita Gentry, to forget he had been in love with her, but he never had. Whenever he met a woman he might have had for a wife, he had instinctively compared her to Rita and been dissatisfied. So he kept drifting, aimlessly, unconsciously seeking something he had never found, perhaps could not find. Now Rita was here, flung at him by a perverse fate.

"You haven't married?" he asked. "Or been engaged?"

She turned from the stove. "No. I'm an old maid, Ben. Funny how good men shy off when they know a woman has money." She gave him her back, adding bitterly,

"But there's one thing a man never understands. Money doesn't take the place of a husband."

"I suppose not," he said.

There was silence until she finished the dishes. Sarboe thought of the few hundred dollars he had saved. He looked at his long-fingered hands, skilled in guncraft. He was a good hunter and a good fisherman. He could make a hand on a cattle ranch. That was all. He had little talent for the things Rita valued.

When she was done, she came to the table and sat down. She said coolly, "Roll me a cigarette, Ben." When he gave her a startled look, she laughed softly. "Never mind. I wanted you to see how it is. It's a man's world. I don't claim it's an original discovery, but I have found it out for myself. Well, I propose to live my life the way I want to, and I'll be as respected as any man." She put her hands on the table, closed them and opened them, then asked, "Ben, will you be my partner?"

"The hell! I haven't got anything to offer."

"You have what I lack. Everything. That's why I'm here, really. Maybe you like Mike Kelly, but I know he's a smooth-talking crook as sure as I'm a foot high. He's tied up with George Dallam, and Dallam never did an honest day's work in his life. They'll come here, bring settlers, start a ditch system, and go broke. You know who'll pocket the money?"

"I don't know about Mike."

"I do, Ben. Believe me. I'm not trying to be pious, but I have always gone on the notion that responsibility goes with money. I want to build a town. I'll put in an irrigation system that will be a good one. When I promise settlers a foot of water, they'll get a foot of water, not a dry lateral."

Sarboe said nothing. What she said about Kelly might be true, for he was a little too smooth with the talk. But

Sarboe knew nothing at all about Dallam, and according to Kelly, Dallam was putting up the money.

"Ben, I'll admit one thing right now," Rita went on. "There are a few things no woman can do. Those are your jobs. You said you had nothing to offer. Now listen. You have the location for a town. You have a talent for managing men." She leaned forward, her eyes pinned on his face. "And you're honest. That's important."

He rolled a smoke, not knowing what to say. Ambition had stirred in him at times, but he had no talent for money-making, and it took money to do the big things that a man reaches for in his dreams. Now Rita was shoving the opportunity at him, this girl he had loved as a boy, this girl he had carried in his heart for so many years. He'd be a fool to turn her down. Still, he hesitated, for he would be the tail that the dog would wag, an idea that went against his grain.

"Forget I'm a woman," Rita urged. "Let's put our cards face up and look at them. We have the opportunity of a lifetime right here on the Deschutes. We'll put your savvy and my capital together. In a new country like this, the sky's the limit."

He rose and laid the unlighted cigarette on the table. He walked around the room, trying to see past the forks of the road which lay before him. He said, more to gain time than anything else, "I kind of hate to see these changes come. It's been mighty good fishing on the river."

"I forgot you were the old man of the mountains." She got up and walked around the table to him. "Ben, you're too good a man to waste your life fishing. Don't you want to do something worthwhile?"

"Trouble is, worthwhile things stir hell up," he said somberly. "It's like Kelly said in his letter, though. Progress is moving in."

She nodded. "But remember there's two kinds of progress. You and I are alike in that way. We don't want any part of Kelly's."

"All right," he said. "I guess it's a deal."

"No guessing, Ben. If we go into this, we go all the way. There'll be a fight. You'll have to handle it. That's your part of the partnership."

"I never shied away from a fight. No guessing, Rita. I'll go along."

"That's what I wanted to hear."

He turned to the door, "You can have the bunk. I'll sleep in the barn."

"Fix a bed on the floor. I don't mind your sleeping in here." She laughed lightly. "I mean, we're partners and you're to forget I'm a woman. Besides, I'm the one who should sleep on the floor. I don't like the notion of driving a man out of his bed."

"It's all right. There's plenty of hay left in the barn for a bed."

"Ben," she said softly, "when two people form a partnership, there ought to be something to bind it. It's kind of like, well, christening a ship."

He stopped, one hand on the door knob, not understanding. She came to him, smiling. "You're slow, Ben. I'll show you." She put her hands on his shoulders and kissed him. Then she tilted her head back, laughing. "You see? Now the partnership's legal. Good night."

He mumbled "Good night," and went out, closing the door behind him. He looked up at the sky and the pines waving in the breeze, tall black shapes in the night. Aloud, he said, "She tells me to forget she's a woman and then she kisses me. What kind of sense is that?" He walked to the barn, shaking his head. Then he said, "Why hell, that's just like a woman."

Chapter III

MAD MAN KELLY

THE DAY AFTER Sarboe returned from Prineville, a town was born on the banks of the Deschutes. There were no skyscrapers, not even a false front. No water main or fire departments or police force. Just one wide street marked by stakes, Sarboe's cabin at its south end, and a total population of two.

"You'll see an amazing increase within a week," Rita said confidently. "Time is the secret of success and we've got the jump on Kelly."

"What are we naming this burg?" Sarboe asked. "Gentryville?"

"Of course not. Maybe you'd like to call it Sarboeburg?"

He grinned. "Now that would be a hell of a name. Try again."

She put a finger to her lips, staring at the river. "It's beautiful. It's not like any other river I've ever seen."

"There aren't any other rivers like it to see," he said. "For one thing, it's the coldest water you ever fell into, even in August. Another thing is it don't vary much. Flows about the same all year."

She nodded. "And it runs north. Not many rivers in the country do that, either." She gestured as if they were wasting time. "We're just being poetic or something. The only thing the settlers will be interested in is whether there's enough water to raise crops."

He grinned. "Well, let's call it Plenty Water. Or Big Ditch City."

She wasn't listening. Her eyes were on the river where it curled out of the pine forest to make a sweeping bend here along the edge of Sarboe's meadow. "Ben, most of our settlers will be coming from Kansas and Nebraska where they've been burned out year after year. We've got to think of a name that will make them want to come here."

"Bonanza," he suggested. "New Jerusalem. Paradise." He winked at her. "How about Big Dew?"

"Ben, you're being silly. I tell you water is the answer, and in bigger amounts than dew. It's here, flowing the same day after day, so swiftly that . . ."

"Swift River."

"Swift River." She turned to him, her face radiant. "That's it, Ben. Swift River, the city of promise on the banks of the Deschutes. Why, I could kiss you for thinking of that name."

"Go ahead."

"It was just an expression, Mr. Sarboe," she said severely. "Remember you're forgetting that I'm a woman."

"You make it hard to forget," he told her.

She was staring at Deschutes, saying softly, "Swift River," as if enjoying the feel of the words on her lips. She turned to him again. "Ben, when does the stage go through?"

He glanced at his watch. "It's three. He was due an hour ago, but the roads are soft . . ."

"I've got to write a letter." She ran to the cabin, calling back, "If he comes before I'm done, make him wait. This letter has to go out today."

Puzzled, he watched her until she disappeared into the cabin. He had a feeling that more of this had been planned in Rita Gentry's mind than she was letting on. Shrugging, he followed to the cabin and waited outside. For several minutes he stood listening to the scratching of her pen on the paper, then she appeared in the doorway, sealing the envelope.

"Where's the mail sack?"

He motioned to the sack hanging from a nail driven into a log outside the door. "Right there. If I'm not around, Barney grabs it, drops his, and goes on."

"Why, anyone could steal it."

"Yeah, we'll sure have to change that, now that progress is coming. You see, up to now there hasn't been anyone around who would steal it, and nobody ever sent anything out that was worth stealing."

"Still the old man of the mountains," she jeered. "Here, mail my letter."

Taking the envelope from her, he saw that it was addressed to John Meacham, The Dalles, Oregon. The stage was coming then. Sarboe took the sack off the nail and dropped the letter into it. The coach stopped in front of the cabin, Barney Johns' eyes on Rita as he threw a mail sack down and grabbed the one Sarboe tossed him.

"How's the weather in Silver Lake?" Sarboe asked.

"Warming up. Getting warmer here, too, ain't it?"

"A little. Barney, meet Rita Gentry, my partner. We're starting a new town here."

"How are you, Barney?" Rita smiled at him. "Long run to Shaniko, isn't it?"

"Quite a run." Barney raised his wide-brimmed hat. "Yes ma'am, quite a run. Maybe you're right about staying, Ben. Damned if this country don't look better all of a sudden. I reckon this here town of yours will grow mighty fast as soon as I tell folks what I seen down here."

"Spread the good word," Rita said, still smiling. "Swift River will be the biggest town in Central Oregon. You'll see.'"

"Well now, Prineville's got an edge on you, but it ain't got the attractions you've got. No siree. Well, got to roll. See you last of the week."

The coach creaked on past the cabin and disappeared into the pines. Sarboe glanced at Rita. He said, "Why didn't you bring somebody along? Don't look right, you staying with me."

"I'm not worrying, Ben. Not about myself. I told you I'd live here the way I want to live."

"Who's John Meacham?"

"A newspaper man. He's in The Dalles waiting until he gets that letter telling him we're ready to go. He'll send some stories out to Willamette Valley towns. Maybe back to the Middle West. Then he'll head up here with his press. Meanwhile we've got to get some buildings up. I expect my crew in this evening."

"You mean you've already got them started up here?"

"Certainly. We left Shaniko yesterday morning, but I came on ahead. I had to fix it with you."

"Mighty sure of yourself," he said indignantly.

"You have to be if you want to make a dream come true." She laid a hand on his arm, her eyes searching his face. "I've dreamed about this for a long time, Ben. When I found out from Kelly that you were here, I got things started. I knew I could make you see things my way. I had to."

"Sure," he said, and let it go at that.

Rita's men did get in that evening, a dozen wagons of them. She ran out of the cabin when she heard them, waving and crying a greeting. The man in the lead wagon waved his hat in a great circle above his head and let out a squall. He yelled, "I told you we'd be in tonight."

"Right on the dot," she shouted.

Later she brought him to the cabin. Fred Purvane, she said his name was. An engineer and the best in the business. His job was to stake out the townsite and dig the ditch.

Purvane shook hands with Sarboe, coolly sizing him up. Purvane was a lanky man, perhaps thirty-five, Sarboe judged, with a network of lines around his eyes and a lantern-jawed face that seemed inordinately melancholy. He said, "I'll get that ditch dug if you keep Dallam off my neck. I don't claim to be no fighter." He jerked a thumb at Rita. "She says you are."

"I'll do what I can," Sarboe said.

"It'll take a piece of doing. Dallam will figure we're moving in on his territory. Now I don't know about this man Kelly, but I do know Dallam. He ain't gonna like it. No sir, he won't like it a little bit."

Rita had asked Purvane to stay for supper. Now, busy at the stove, she gave Sarboe a quick glance. "Ben, I was just thinking. We don't have a law officer of any kind and we're a long ways from Prineville. Don't you think the sheriff would appoint a deputy for this end of the county when he finds out what's happening?"

"Maybe somebody who would sort of see things our way," Purvane added. "I tell you, Sarboe, there ain't a mean trick in the book that George Dallam don't know. Wouldn't surprise me none if he wrote the book."

Rita frowned at him. "We don't want any favors, Fred. We just want the peace kept."

"All right." Sarboe nodded. "I'll go over tomorrow and see if I can talk the sheriff out of a star."

"Buy some hay while you're there," Rita said. "All the lumber you can get, too. Hire the hauling done. We'll need our teams here. And what about those steers you bought for Kelly?"

Sarboe grinned ruefully. "No sense giving our competition a boost. I'll see if I can get 'em over here right away. We'll eat 'em ourselves."

Later, when the meal was finished, Purvane scooted back his chair. "Let's get a whiff of this fine air you've got, Sarboe." He lifted a cigar from his pocket. "I want a smoke anyhow."

"When did you start going outside to smoke?" Rita demanded.

"Just since I got here. You know, Rita, the air up here is so damned thin that a cigar just don't draw good in the house."

She shook her fist at him, laughing. "All right. Get outside and do your gabbing, but I want a full account when you get back."

Sarboe followed the engineer outside, puzzled. Purvane fired his cigar and moved across the meadow toward the river. The night chill was in the air now, and Purvane shivered. He said, "Sarboe, I've got a hunch I'll freeze to death before I ever get that ditch finished."

They walked on, Sarboe remaining silent. At the lower end of the clearing campfires made red holes in the blackness. The wagons bulked darkly at the edge of the timber, and man talk came to Sarboe, the words flowing together into an indistinguishable blur of sound.

"The boys have a rest coming," Purvane said. "We didn't waste no time getting here. Couldn't tell what Rita would run into."

Silence again except for the whispering rush of the river and the run of talk from the fires. Sarboe could not guess what was on Purvane's mind. His face was a long wedge in the blackness, the glow of his cigar vividly red when he drew on it, then fading as he let it rest.

The silence ribboned out and grew strained, Purvane apparently willing to let it ride for a time. Then, unable to stand it any longer, Sarboe burst out, "Purvane, did you bring me out here just to listen to the river?"

"No. I've got a question to ask. No sense beating around the bush. Rita's been using your cabin. Where have you been sleeping?"

Sarboe stood ten feet from the engineer. Now he took a step toward Purvane, hands fisted, anger clawing up through him. But he took only one step, for he was not a man to let his anger rule him. He said, "In the barn, if it's any of your damned business."

"Rita's business is my business," Purvane said. "You don't remember me, but I was working for Cal Gentry when you were in Cripple Creek. Our paths didn't cross, me being in the mine and you outside. You didn't stay long, or chances are we would have met. Your leaving was smart, you and Rita being just kids like you were. I've been with her since Cal died, giving her a hand with everything she's tried. She'd have gone broke before now if I hadn't.''

"Maybe you'd better tell me where you've been sleeping," Sarboe said sharply.

"A fair question," Purvane admitted reasonably. "She's straight, Sarboe. Don't get any other notion. I just wanted to find out what kind of hairpin you are. You see . . ." He hesitated, pulling hard on his cigar, and then added, his voice sour with disappointment, "I never said this to nobody before, but if you're smart, you'll see why I'm saying it to you. I love Rita, but she won't have me, so I just trail along, trying to be satisfied with a smile when all the time I'm wanting a hell of a lot more. But I'll see her treated right. Don't never forget that.''

"We won't do no fighting over her," Sarboe said. "She made a proposition and I took it.''

"Her money and organization against your quarter section and gun savvy. You got the best of it, friend.''

"It was her idea," Sarboe said hotly. "Likewise she said to forget she was a woman.''

Purvane laughed shortly. "Can you do that? Or any man?''

"No, I reckon not," Sarboe admitted, "but it was the way she wanted it.''

Purvane turned toward the cabin. "She's got a tough crust, but don't let that fool you. She wants the same things any woman does. She's just a little longer on pride than most women are.'' He threw his cigar away, sparks flying as it hit the ground. "And don't figure you've taken on an easy job. It calls for a hell of a lot more than a fast gun, and I don't aim to let Rita go broke on this. I wasn't in favor of the move, but she had her head set.''

Rita was drying dishes when they went into the cabin. She made a half turn, the lamplight falling upon her amber-gold hair. She said "I suppose you boys worked me over.''

"No," Purvane said. "I was just impressing on this bucko that he's got a tough job. I'll mosey along. Sarboe can eat breakfast with us."

"I don't mind . . ."

"Sure," Sarboe said, "but there's no use of you getting up that early."

For a moment Purvane stood with his hand on the door, a half smile on his long lips, eyes on Rita as if he could not get enough of the sight of her. He said then, "Good night," and went out.

Sarboe remained for a moment, watching Rita. Last night he had been sure he was still in love with her. Now he wondered. It wasn't like it used to be when her presence sent a fire roaring through him.

She finished the last dish and turned toward him. She was wearing the same dress she had worn the day before; her hair was not as neatly pinned as she had kept it all day, and there was a smudge of flour along one cheek. She dropped into a chair, saying, "Sit down, Ben."

He shook his head. "I'll roll in, too. Got a lot of riding to do tomorrow."

She put her elbows on the table and, lacing her fingers together, lowered her chin upon them. She asked, "What did Fred tell you about me?"

He hesitated, thinking how a man's past can come back to plague him. Rita Gentry was nothing like the girl he had known in Cripple Creek, nor was he the Ben Sarboe she had known. The years had brought their changes. A man could not take up where he had left off just as if those years had never been.

Now he wondered if he had made a mistake throwing in with her. She was proud, she was capable, and she had a talent for controlling the actions of men who worked with her. There was nothing wrong with those qualities and he could respect her for them, but the truth of the matter was that he had thrown away his freedom when he had given her his word. Now that knowledge galled him.

"Nothing bad," he said at last. "It was just surprising, him telling me he was working for Cal the same time I was."

"I should have told you, but it doesn't make any difference. I mean, as far as we're concerned. Fred's a sort of big brother. Kind of annoying at times." She smiled. "But he's helped me and I'm grateful."

"Purvane's all right. Well, I'll see you the last of the week. I'll be over there a few days."

"You won't know Swift River when you get back," she told him.

He said, "Good night," and went out. She was still sitting at the table when he closed the door, smiling, chin resting on her laced fingers.

Sarboe was in Prineville three days. He had no trouble buying hay and lumber; he found men with teams and wagons who were glad to have work. The rancher from whom he had bought the steers promised to deliver them the first of the week. Those were the easy things to do and he did them first. He put off seeing the sheriff until the last morning he was in town.

The lawman was an Ochoco Creek cattleman who had left the management of his ranch to his sons while he served his term. He was a good man for the job although Sarboe heard he wore his star with some reluctance, having run for office only because the public demanded it.

The sheriff nodded approval the instant Sarboe told him he was willing to serve as deputy. "You say you've has some experience as a lawman?"

"Not around here. In the Southwest."

"Don't make no difference. You've smelled more powder smoke than I'll ever smell." The sheriff scratched his nose. "Why ain't you packing a gun?"

"Haven't needed one since I came to the Deschutes."

"Well, you will now because you won't have to beg me for a star. I've heard a lot about you and it's all been good. Fact is, I'm glad to get a deputy over there. We all figured that country would be settled sooner or later, but I kind of hate to see it. They'll want their own county, and that'll split Crook County right down the middle.''

The sheriff dug around in a desk drawer until he found a star and then he swore Sarboe in. He said, "Handle anything that comes up if you can. If you need help, just holler.''

"I'll do that," Sarboe said, and left the sheriff's office.

He was not, Sarboe thought as he rode up the steep grade west of Crooked River, in an altogether happy situation. Purvane had said frankly that it would be a good idea to have a deputy who would see things their way, but Rita had said they didn't want any favors. Still, it could amount to the same thing. If Mike Kelly and George Dallam made trouble, Deputy Ben Sarboe would have to do something about it.

Reaching the rim, Sarboe pulled his horse up to let him blow and looked down into the valley. Ochoco Creek flowed into Crooked River and spring was beginning to give its emerald touch to the land along the streams. To the east were the Blue Mountains, westward beyond the Deschutes was the Cascade range, both rich with the finest stand of yellow pine that Sarboe had ever seen.

Here, to the west of where Sarboe sat in his saddle, was a vast stretch of good soil, an ample water supply, mature timber ready to be harvested. There would be a railroad, screaming saws, stacks of new yellow lumber, mountains of sawdust, a haze of smoke blurring the sun, a wasteland of stumps for miles along the river. There would be farmers living in tarpaper shacks grubbing out sagebrush and junipers, ditches running bankfull, fields sharply green instead of desert gray.

Again Sarboe felt the tug of conflict within him, for there was both a right and wrong to this, and the wrong was the price that Americans continually paid for what they called progress.

"Old man of the mountains, she says," Sarboe muttered. "Hell, I'll wind up being an empire builder.''

It was late afternoon with the sun settling down toward the Three Sisters when Sarboe rode into the meadow that had been his home for a year and now was the site of Swift River. Even before he came out of the timber he heard the clean, ringing blows of ax on pine, the shout of teamsters, the song of crosscut saws. Still, he was unprepared for what he saw.

During the few days that he had been gone, Swift River had become something more than a street marked by stakes. A dozen cabins had been built. Tents were up all over the townsite, and a small army of men were laboring with the industriousness of ants.

Rita saw Sarboe the instant he rode into the clearing. She ran toward him, crying something and waving, and he touched up his roan. Then she reached him and he pulled his horse to a stop, her frantic words beating against his ears. "Ben, Mike Kelly's here."

Surprised, he said, "It ain't the first of May."

"He's here anyhow. He heard what we were doing. A man named Verd Ricket got word to him." Rita gulped, struggling with her breathing for a moment before she could go on. "Ricket came after his mail the morning you left. Wanted to know what was going on and I told him. He said he thought Kelly was putting in an irrigation project and I said that you and I were partners. Then he asked me where Kelly was and I said The Dalles. He must have ridden up there and told Kelly."

Sarboe stepped down, thinking quickly of this. Verd Ricket had put two and two together and, sensing the possibility of trouble, had touched a match to the fuse. Sarboe said, "I guess it don't make no big difference."

"It might, Ben." She gripped his arm. "We aren't ready for trouble yet. I was counting on more time."

Suddenly Sarboe was aware of the silence. Men had dropped axes and saws and were crowding into the street. Fred Purvane was there, long face more melancholy than ever. Then Sarboe saw Mike Kelly striding toward him. He was a big man, this Mike Kelly, nearly a head taller than Sarboe, with a nest of freckles on a fat nose, and now his square face seemed almost as red as his hair.

The summer before Sarboe had known Kelly as a good-humored man with a loud voice and a roaring laugh. Now he saw that this was a different Kelly, gripped by savage, killing rage.

"It's about time you were showing up," Kelly bawled. "When I wrote to you about my plans, I didn't figure you'd sell me out."

Sarboe had not taken his gun with him. Now he saw that a Colt rode on Kelly's right hip, and he knew at once that this might be rough. He said softly, "Get back, Rita," and stood there beside his horse while Kelly came to a stop five feet from him, great legs spread.

Chapter IV

THE LINES ARE DRAWN

SARBOE did not know Mike Kelly, not this Mike Kelly who stood before him. The man had gone past the place where his actions would be controlled by reason; he was a creature of violent emotion. Sarboe knew he could prevent trouble if he had time, but there was no time. Ordinarily the man was not a killer, but gripped as he was now by a violent temper, he was capable of anything.

"Welcome to Swift River," Sarboe said, very mild.

He took a step forward, right hand extended. Kelly, surprised at this apparent friendliness, stood motionless. Then Sarboe exploded into swift and unexpected action. His left shoulder jammed into Kelly's chest, and at the same time his right hand swept Kelly's gun from leather.

Kelly cursed and swung on Sarboe, but Sarboe ducked and stepping back, tossed the gun across the street. He said, "Now we can talk, Mike. I don't favor gabbing with a man who's hot under the collar when he's got a gun and I ain't."

"To hell with you," Kelly bawled. "I'll do no talking with you this day."

Kelly lunged at him, feinting with his left, right driving for Sarboe's face. He missed, and Sarboe, coming in fast, caught him on the side of the head and knocked him flat into the deep dust of the newly graded street. He jumped up and moved forward again, this time more deliberately.

Sarboe was a smaller man than Kelly, but he was faster and he was hard to hit. He caught Kelly in the stomach, jolted him with a short right that flattened his freckled nose, and cracked him in the chest. He danced away, weaving and turning, boots stirring the dust. Kelly stormed after him, panting, blood streaming down his face from his battered nose. He threw his left that missed and Sarboe tried with a right that Kelly took on a shoulder.

There was a wild flurry of action with Sarboe pressing the fight now and Kelly trying to cover up. He began backing away, not liking this for he was being hurt. Then Sarboe stepped into a hole and stumbled. He was momentarily off balance and in that same instant Kelly caught him with a long looping blow that knocked him flat.

Sarboe rolled; he glimpsed Kelly start a big foot that would have smashed his ribs if it had struck him. He rolled again, angry now, and came to his feet. Kelly rushed, apparently thinking that Sarboe was badly hurt. Overanxious, he left himself open and Sarboe hit him with right and left, in the stomach and in the face and in the stomach again.

The last blow did the job; it slammed the wind out of Kelly and brought his guard down. Sarboe stepped in close and drove a whistling right squarely to the point of his chin. Kelly folded into the dust and rolled over on his face and lay still.

Stepping back, Sarboe sleeved sweat and dirt from his face. He shook his head; he was a little dizzy and he had been hurt by the one hard blow that Kelly had landed. Rita was beside him then, holding to his arm and asking, "You all right, Ben?"

"Sure, sure," he said. "I'm all right."

Purvane was there, saying excitedly, "He'd have killed you, Sarboe, if you hadn't got his gun. I tell you him and George Dallam are two of a kind."

"Maybe." Sarboe motioned toward Kelly. "Have a couple of your boys tote him over to the cabin."

"What for?" Purvane demanded. "You'd be a damned sight smarter if you'd kick his . . ."

"Do what I tell you," Sarboe said.

He walked across the street to where he had thrown Kelly's gun. He picked it up and slipped it into his waistband, and when he turned, he saw that two of Purvane's men were carrying Kelly toward his cabin. Rita was still standing where Sarboe had left her, worried eyes pinned on him.

He moved back to her. "I'm going to talk to him. Want to listen?"

"It's a waste of time talking to him, Ben. He was crazy mad when he rode in here. Said some things I'd like to forget."

"Probably been storing them up ever since Verd Ricket saw him. Maybe he's got a right to feel that way."

She shook her head. "We've done nothing wrong, Ben. I tell you I know George Dallam. He's the kind who will cheat . . ."

"I'm going to talk to Kelly, not Dallam," Sarboe said roughly, and turning, walked toward his cabin.

Rita fell into step beside him, her face showing strong disapproval. Anger stirred in Sarboe. He was having his way now, but judging from the look on Rita's face, he'd hear about it later. She was not convinced and neither was Purvane. A partnership was a matter of balance. It could not work if either partner carried too much weight, and he had a feeling that it was a point Rita had never considered.

Kelly was sitting at the table when Sarboe came into the cabin. One of Purvane's men had gone, the other stood watching the sullen Kelly. Sarboe said, "Get his horse." He walked to the stove, sloshed water into a basin and set it on the table.

"Go to hell," Kelly muttered. "Soon as that horse gets here, I'm riding."

"Not yet you ain't. Sarboe tossed a towel to the table. "You're a mess. Get some of the blood off your mug. You ain't real pretty for a lady to look at."

Kelly raised his eyes to Rita who stood in the doorway. He said, "A lady?"

"Mike," Sarboe said, "I'll tell you something. You say that again and what I just done won't be a start to what I will do."

Kelly got up and grabbed the edge of the table till the dizziness passed. He washed, being careful not to touch his nose, and picked up a towel and dried. He sat down again, glaring at Sarboe.

"Let's get this straight, Mike," Sarboe said. "You've got no cause to be sore. You sent a letter telling me what to do. Strikes me you took a hell of a lot for granted."

"I had a right to," Kelly stormed. "This development was my idea. Took all winter to talk Dallam into backing me. Now you and this — this Miss Gentry beat me out of it."

"We didn't beat you out of nothing. Rita came along with a partnership offer, which is more'n you done. Any fool would make the best deal he could. Or maybe you've forgotten this quarter section is mine."

"His horse is here, Ben," Rita said from the doorway.

Kelly rose. "Give me my gun."

"No hurry. We've got no reason to fight, Mike. You didn't give me any choice today."

"And you didn't give me any. If I'd had a chance to have used my gun . . ."

"I wasn't heeled, but you'd have burned me down. That it?"

"You're damned right," Kelly said hotly, "but there'll be another time as sure as you're a foot high."

"And you'll hang." Sarboe gestured wearily. "What's got into you, Mike? This ain't so important. Go find yourself another river. Or go downstream and dig your ditch."

"That's just what we will do. We'll fight, too. There isn't room for both of us here. We'll fight you to hell and back, and before we're done, you'll wish a thousand times you'd played with me instead of her."

"You see, Ben," Rita said.

Sarboe unloaded the gun and handed it to Kelly. "The next time you come back we'll have a jail for gents like you who tote guns in town."

"Town." Kelly snorted his derision. "You won't have no town, Ben. You'll never have nothing but stakes and tents and a few cabins. In a year from now you won't even have that. We'll have a town, me and George Dallam, and it'll be here a hundred years from now."

Kelly stood with one hand on the table, his battered face ugly with fury. Sarboe thought of the Mike Kelly he had known and liked, Mike Kelly with the great laugh and his dreams about the future of the country, Mike Kelly who had slept in his cabin and eaten at this table and who had broken the monotony of lonely living for Sarboe through most of last summer.

"I'm sorry," Sarboe said. "I want no fight."

"You'll have one. That's a promise."

Kelly moved to the door, reeling uncertainly. Rita stepped aside. Kelly gripped the jamb and clung there, breathing hard, one hand coming up to his eyes.

"You don't have to ride yet, Mike," Sarboe said.

"To hell with you," he muttered, and went to his horse.

For a moment Kelly stood with one hand holding the saddle horn, then he pulled himself into leather and drawing his gun, fumbled shells from his belt and reloaded. Sarboe took his gun belt down from the wall and buckled it around him.

"I wouldn't try what you're thinking, Mike," Sarboe said.

Kelly held the gun in front of him, head turned so he could watch both Sarboe and Rita. He said, "It's like I told you. There'll be another time. Then I'll be finding out if you're as tough as she lets on." He jerked a thumb at Rita. "I doubt like hell that you are."

A sickness crawled up into Sarboe. He had seven years of this after he'd left Cripple Creek, then he'd had a year of peace. One year. No more. Now it was over. He said, dry-lipped, "I'm the law here on the river, Mike. Don't forget that."

"And it's damned crooked law we'll have. We'll see about that, too."

Kelly shoved his gun into the holster and rode away, one hand still clutching the saddle horn. He rode bent forward, swaying a little as if he had all he could do to stay on his horse. Sarboe watched him until he had ridden the length of the street and disappeared into the pines. Then he looked at Rita. "You were right today, but maybe he'll be of a mind to talk when he gets over his mad. I'll try again."

She shook her head. "I know how you feel, Ben. You want to think of Kelly as a friend and it's hard to lose a friend. But you've already lost him."

"I won't lose him. He was out of his head today." Sarboe motioned toward the river. "Hell, there's enough water in the Deschutes to irrigate two segregations. Or a dozen. It ain't that I'm trying to duck trouble. It's just that there ain't no reason for it."

"Plenty of reason if you know Dallam like Fred and I do, and remember that if Kelly wanted to be fair, he'd have offered you a partnership."

"Yeah, I know," Sarboe admitted.

She smiled. "Well, let's forget it for tonight, Ben. We'll go ahead with our plans and we can't stop them from going ahead with theirs. Now I'll get supper started. I expect you're starved."

"My tapeworm's hollering for a fact," he said. "Guess I'll go fishing. Trout for breakfast. How does that sound?"

"Wonderful."

But it was not Sarboe's evening to go fishing. He had a dozen strikes and missed them all. His mind was on Mike Kelly. Rita thought she understood how it was with them, but she didn't. To Ben Sarboe the ties of friendship had always been strong, so strong that now he began to wonder how much of this break with Kelly was his fault. When Rita called supper, he went back to the cabin, empty-handed, still wondering.

Chapter V

HEART AND MIND

FROM THE DAY that Ben Sarboe had left Cripple Creek there had been a constant tug in Rita between her heart and her mind. At first it had been one-sided, for her heart had been the stronger. She had loved Sarboe with all the fervency that is in a strong-minded seventeen-year-old girl who had never failed to gain anything she had really wanted. She had always been able to bend her father to her wishes, so she had never asked him what he thought of Sarboe. She knew they got along and her father respected him. At the time it had seemed enough.

So she had gone along day after day, thinking and planning and dreaming about her life with Sarboe, assuming that he loved her, that he'd go on working for her father, and that some day he'd get around to asking her to marry him. Then he was gone without a word of explanation or good-bye.

At first she had been hurt, then bitterly angry, and she had told herself a thousand times that she hated Ben Sarboe. But the years had matured her. Gradually her mind had grown until it outweighed her heart. Sarboe had become less important in her thinking until she thought she neither hated nor loved him.

As she had told Sarboe, she had purposely set out to make a place for herself in a man's world. She had learned that common sense, money, and men like Fred Purvane who were loyal to her made a winning combination, and she had gradually come to expect both loyalty and obedience from the men who worked for her as casually as she expected the sun to come up each morning. She had given little thought to anything as ephemeral as love until Mike Kelly had told her Ben Sarboe was here on the Deschutes. Then she felt a tingle go down her spine. Instinctively she had made her decision.

Now, sitting across from Sarboe at the table, she did not regret that decision, but she realized with sudden alarm that this was going to be a harder job than she had anticipated. Her heart was back in the saddle again and she knew that her cool, common-sense judgment would not be as cool as it had been. She could not be sure of Sarboe as she was sure of Purvane; she sensed an inner strength in him that set him apart from other men.

It had been a long time since Rita had done any housework. She had never learned to be a fancy cook, the things her father had contemptuously called "gape and swaller," but she knew what men liked, plain food like ham, potatoes, gravy, biscuits and coffee, and that was what she had put on the table. It gave her pleasure to watch Sarboe eat, and the realization of that pleasure stirred a new worry in her. She would not be reduced to a housekeeper.

She rose and filled Sarboe's coffee cup. He had cleaned up the ham and eaten the last biscuit. Now he sat back to roll a cigarette, utterly content. He said, "Good meal."

"Thanks, Ben. Maybe you were just hungry."

He shook his head. "No. You're a good cook. Looking at you helps, too."

"You've been alone too long. It isn't good for a man to live without a woman, you know."

"That's right, I guess." He fired his cigarette. "Well, it's like you said. My vacation's over." He tipped his chair back against the wall, frowning. "I'm a lawman again, toting a star and a gun, but I'm a businessman at the same time. Before we're done, they won't jibe."

She stood with her back to the stove, her hands behind her. They seemed cold and that was crazy because the fire was burning briskly. For a moment she said nothing, her eyes on him. He had changed a great deal, more than she had wanted to admit to herself. His features were the same: the wide nose and resolute mouth and square chin with the deep cleft. His curly brown hair was exactly as she had remembered, the white crescent-shaped scar was still there on the left side of his jaw.

She would have known him anywhere because his looks had not changed. The change was inside him. In Cripple Creek he had been easygoing except when he had been forced into a fight. He had thought nothing of losing a month's wages over the poker table. He often drank more than he should. He hadn't told her, but she sensed that those were things he would do sparingly now, or not at all.

"They'll jibe all right," she said uneasily. "I mean, I don't think it's anything to worry about. Not now anyhow."

"Maybe not." He rose and tossed his cigarette stub into the fire. "I've been wondering just what my part of the business is. I ain't much when it comes to cutting down trees and building cabins and digging ditches."

"You don't have to do those things," she said quickly. "It's like Fred says. You keep Dallam off Purvane's neck and he'll see that the ditch gets dug."

"Then I'll keep busy fishing. That it?"

They were on dangerous ground now and she did not want this to come to a clash of wills. She said carefully, "No use fishing unless you do better than you did tonight."

"I will. The trout were just faster'n I was." He gestured as if dismissing anything as unimportant as fish. "I was thinking about something else today. About you and me."

She felt that old familiar tingle go down her back again. She had forgotten about it through the years after he had left Cripple Creek until she had heard he was here.

"What about us, Ben?" she asked softly.

" 'Bout us being partners. Take this Mike Kelly business. You keep saying there's no use to talk to him. You didn't want me to talk to him after our ruckus."

Something died inside her. She had thought he was going to say something very different from that, and now she hated herself for the thought. She was soft, as soft and giddy as she'd been at seventeen. It wouldn't do, not for the Rita Gentry she was now.

She said, her tone sharp, "But you did talk to him."

"Yeah, only you didn't like it. Now I aim to find him tomorrow and see if I can do any better." He kicked absently at the woodbox. "You still won't like it. So I got to thinking about partnerships. I reckon a lot of 'em bust up because the partners don't get along. We don't want ours to work that way."

"Well?"

"That's what got me to thinking. It strikes me that after Cal died and you started to run your business, you sort of got into the habit of giving orders. Maybe I done the same. Most lawmen do.'' He kicked at the woodbox again. ''So it seemed to me it would be a good idea to figure out which things you'd give the orders on and what I'd give 'em on.''

She felt her nerves tighten. This was something she should have thought about. The partnership was her idea. She had been perfectly willing to share the profits equally with him, but the thought that Sarboe would be giving some of the orders had not occurred to her.

''I guess I don't see just what you're driving at,'' she said. ''I think we should talk over anything that's important.''

He grinned at her. ''Sure, but after we get done talking, we've still got to decide what we're going to do, and it's purty plain that we ain't always gonna decide the same way.''

''What was your idea?''

''Well, I sort of cotton to the notion of dividing things up. You and Purvane know how to dig a ditch and sell a townsite. I don't, so you can have your head on them things, but trouble is my business. I'd better do the deciding on that.''

She knew he was right. Still, a sudden and illogical perverseness was in her. After all, he owed her something, going off the way he had that time. He had owed it to her for eight years, and she had waited a long time to collect.

''I don't know about that,'' she said. ''There's no room in our business for sentiment. I found out years ago that there's only one way to handle trouble.''

They stood quite close, facing each other. She was aware of a number of extraneous things, that she was almost as tall as he was, that alongside his hard-muscled body hers was very slender. She was aware, too, that he was grinning as if what she had just said was a joke, and it infuriated her.

"I've been called a lot of things," Sarboe said, "but I don't think anybody ever said I was sentimental before." He shook his head, the grin leaving his mouth. "It ain't a proposition of sentiment, Rita. There's two ways to treat trouble. One is to sit on the seat of your pants till it hits you. The other way is to head it off. I've found that's the best."

"But you can't head this off, Ben. Dallam's just plain no good. Kelly's no better or he wouldn't have thrown in with Dallam. I say the only way to handle men like that is to lick hell out of them."

She had spoken loudly, too loudly, and suddenly she sensed that she had shown her weakness in that blustering tone. Panic threatened to sweep over her. She had never worked with a man she couldn't manage. It had been simple before this. When she found she had a man on her hands that she couldn't manage, she fired him. But she couldn't fire Sarboe and she wouldn't have wanted to if she could. So it was a challenge, and she needed time to learn how to meet it.

"We may have to if it comes to that," Sarboe said, "but we'll give my way a try first."

Turning from her, he walked across the room to where he had dropped his hat on a bench. His tone had been final. He had offered her a compromise. She should have taken it. She cried out, "Ben, we don't have to decide this tonight. We can work our way out of this by doing things as we go along."

He picked up his hat. "No. We'd better get started right. Tomorrow I'm taking a ride down the river to see Kelly. Maybe it'll be a waste of time like you said, maybe not, but I aim to try."

He opened the door and would have gone out then if she hadn't said, "Ben, I feel awful about running you out of your cabin this way, but we're starting work on the hotel tomorrow. As soon as I can, I'll take a room there."

"No hurry. This cabin ain't much, but you're sure welcome to it. You don't have to cook for me, neither. That wasn't in the bargain."

"I'd like to, Ben," she said quickly.

He shook his head. "You've got plenty to do, and I oughtta be eating with your outfit. Don't look quite right the way we're doing." He stepped outside, said, "So long, Rita," and shut the door.

"So long, Ben," she said, and knew he did not hear.

She filled the firebox and set a pan of water on the front of the stove to heat. She stood in the center of the room looking around at the bare walls, the crude table and chairs and bench, the shelves of food and dishes and pans, the mail rack near the door. So far she had done nothing to change his cabin. It was a man's place, clean and neat enough, but definitely a man's home. She would leave it that way.

She stacked the dishes, thinking of women she had known who gave themselves to their men, scrubbing and cooking and washing, bearing their husbands' children, submerging themselves until they lost their individuality. She would not do that. It was something she had often said she would never do and she mentally said it again. That sort of life was for other women, not Rita Gentry.

She began washing the dishes, feeling again a dissatisfaction that had long been in her. At twenty-five she had no living kin. If she died tomorrow, there would be no one who would feel any great loss or sorrow. Oh, she'd be missed all right, missed by men like Fred Purvane who had worked for her for a long time. The routine of their lives would be changed; they would have to find other jobs, and some might even feel a pang of regret. That would be all.

When her father had died she had lost the sense of belonging to someone. It was the price she paid to live the life she wanted just as the other women who so completely gave themselves to their men paid a price for their lost freedom. She had known some who seemed very happy. It had been a long time since she had been really happy, and now she wondered who was the wiser.

It was something she had not thought of before, and it brought an uneasiness to her. She tried to put it out of her mind. She had always been proud of her strength and her accomplishments, her willingness to risk censure in order to live her own life, but somehow she could not regain the sense of satisfaction that was usually in her. Ben Sarboe had done that to her.

There was a knock on the door and she crossed the room, hoping that Sarboe had returned, but when she opened the door she saw that it was Fred Purvane. Masking her disappointment, she said, "Howdy, Fred. Come in."

She stepped aside and he came in, his hat in his hand. "Can't stay long," he said apologetically, "but I wanted to talk to you a minute. I aim to line out the ditch tomorrow."

She motioned to a chair. "Sit down, Fred."

"Can't stay." He rolled the hat brim in his hands, eyes on the floor. "This fellow Sarboe. He handled Kelly pretty well."

Purvane always had a melancholy look about his long-jawed face, and now it seemed more melancholy than ever. She saw that he was embarrassed as if wanting to say something that was hard to put into words. She said, "He really did a job," and waited.

Purvane's eyes swung around the room and touched her face and were lowered again. "He's all you said he was. I reckon he'll take care of Dallam all right. Like the old-timers say, he'll do to take along."

It wasn't Purvane's way to labor like this when he had something on his mind. She said, "Fred, quit beating around the bush."

He gave her a straight look, and then spread his hands as if feeling that what he had to say would be a waste of words. "I ain't one to talk about personal things, Rita, but you know I'd do anything I could for you."

"Why, of course," she said, still puzzled.

Purvane cleared his throat. "Well, now about Sarboe. I've known for a long time you were in love with him."

Shocked, she said, "Am I that easy to read?"

"Just for me. Don't forget I've been around since you were a harum-scarum kid, more boy than girl. Maybe I wasn't real sure about how you felt till Kelly told you Sarboe was here. Then right off you got things to rolling."

"I needed him, Fred."

"Not the way you've needed other men. Me. Or John Meacham. What I'm getting around to saying is that I hope you won't lose your head over him. You can tell a lot about a man by the way he fights. He licked Kelly just like he was chopping down a tree. He didn't have no real feelings about it, and I doubt that he does about anything."

"You're wrong, Fred. Awfully wrong. He has more feeling than you think. He brought Kelly here and talked to him, and he's bent on talking to him again." She forced a smile. "This is kind of funny. I was thinking he was too sentimental for the job."

Purvane snorted. "Don't you think nothing like that. You let him go see Kelly. He knows what he's doing."

"He'll go," she said tartly, "no matter what I say."

"Will he now." A smile took some of the sadness out of Purvane's face. "Maybe it's a good thing. Looks like I didn't have no call to say this."

Without another word he turned and walked out. She stood in the doorway watching him until he disappeared into the darkness. He had waited outside the cabin, she thought, until he was sure Sarboe had gone.

She shut the door and returned to her dishwashing, asking herself why Purvane had come. As he had said, he was not one to talk about personal matters. Then a startling explanation came to her. Maybe Purvane was in love with her! He had been with her a long time, never pushing himself upon her, but he had always been around when she needed him. Perhaps he had hoped that some day she would be aware of him and his feelings, and he had taken this opportunity to strike at Sarboe. She discarded the thought at once. It was not like Purvane.

When she was done with the dishes, she sat idly beside the fire for a time, not wanting to go to bed, but having nothing to do. Again it struck her that most women would have sewing to do. Embroidery. Crocheting. A quilt to tie. She had nothing of the kind. That sort of work had simply never appealed to her.

She rose and began undressing, wondering about tomorrow. In a few days, or weeks at the most, there would be plenty to do, the kind of work she understood and enjoyed. Now everything was in Purvane's hands. Her work would wait until the people began moving in.

It came to her after she was in bed and the light out, this untenable position she had taken. She could have Purvane and she didn't want him: she wanted Sarboe and he didn't want her. Purvane had said he remembered her as a harum-scarum kid, more boy that girl. *Maybe that was the way Sarboe thought of her now.*

She lay on her back, body tense, staring into the blackness, and she began to blame Sarboe. It went back to their days in Cripple Creek. Seventeen and twenty-one, old enough to be in love and get married and have a life together, but he had wanted none of it. So she made a decision there in the darkness of Ben Sarboe's cabin. They were business partners. They would remain exactly that. She had set herself to accomplish one thing in a man's world. It would have to do.

Chapter VI

LINDA KELLY

SARBOE ate breakfast with Purvane and his men in the big dining tent that had been set up just east of the river. There was some boisterous talk and horseplay; a few slapped Sarboe on the back and said, "That was a hell of a good fight yesterday."

It was a good outfit composed mostly of young men willing to give a day's work for a fair day's wages. The spirit was right. That, more than anything else, impressed Sarboe. There was nothing tangible, nothing he could put his fingers on, but the feeling was unmistakable. They'd do a job regardless of Mike Kelly or George Dallam or the devil himself.

When he finished breakfast, he stepped outside into the chill air. The sun was well up in a clear sky, and westward above the pine-green shoulders of the foothills the Three Sisters and Broken Top stood high and massive, their lines sharp against the blue. Overhead, tall pines were stirred by a small wind, and the river, behind Sarboe, talked with steady rhythm as it hurried northward toward the Columbia.

Sarboe stood for a time along the dusty street, watching. A pine went down, slowly at first as if reluctant to bow to saw and ax, then it gathered speed and rushed earthward with a great roar and crackling of broken limbs, and dust spilled up around it. There was the muffled thunder of a stump being blown out of the earth, the banging of hammers as a pine board was nailed into place, the profane yelling of a teamster as he backed his wagon beside a pile of lumber.

A jerk line outfit wheeled by headed for Silver Lake, the driver calling, "Hi-ya, hi-ya, get along," the leaders' bells jingled, dust was stirred by hoofs and wheels. Later, Purvane and his crew of surveyors left town, Purvane lifting a hand to Sarboe as he passed in his buggy. It was activity, solid and well organized. Progress had come to the Deschutes.

Sarboe was so intent in watching and listening that he was not aware Rita had come up until she said, "What do you think of it, Ben?"

He turned to her, touching the brim of his hat. "You've got a good bunch of men. Somebody's done a job of planning, too. Either you or Purvane."

"Purvane," she said. "I take no credit for it. My part comes later."

She stood beside him, her eyes moving from one man to another, and it struck Sarboe that as far as she was concerned, he was just another member of the crew that fitted into her organization. She needed men who were skilled craftsmen with saws and hammers and axes. His tool was a gun. Later, the riffraff would move in as it always did when a big construction job was under way. When it did, he would be as necessary as any freighter or surveyor or carpenter that she had.

He had never seen her prettier, he thought, nor as completely self-possessed. She was wearing a white shirtwaist and dark skirt that made a snug fit over round hips; her amber hair was braided and pinned on the back of her head. If she felt the chill of the morning, she gave no indication of it.

She turned to him, smiling. "Come on. I'll show you our town."

As he moved with her along the street, she pointed out where the hotel would be, the general store, the livery stable, the blacksmith shop, the newspaper office, and presently they came to a log building on the north side of the street.

"Our office," she said, and opened the door.

She stepped inside and he followed, catching at once the good, strong fragrance of new pine lumber. A stove had been set up in the middle of the room, there were several desks and chairs, and a number of filing cabinets along the wall.

Rita moved past the stove to the back of the room, motioning for him to come. He saw then what she wanted to show him, a rectangular sign with tall black letters: SWIFT RIVER DEVELOPMENT COMPANY. Below was another line, SWIFT RIVER TOWNSITE COMPANY, and across the bottom in small letters, GENTRY AND SARBOE.

He turned to her, grinning. "Looks good."

She showed her relief. "I painted it when you were in Prineville, and there was one thing I hadn't thought to ask you about." She took a long breath and pointed to the bottom line. "I don't think I'm more important than you are, but I thought that since the organization was mine and I was putting up the money, it would be all right this way."

He studied the sign a moment and then turned his gaze to her. "Sure it's all right. What are you driving at?"

She bit her lower lip. "I put my name first. Maybe I should have waited to see . . ."

"I ain't kicking," he cut in. "I'm lucky to have my name there at all."

"I'm glad, Ben." She was able to smile then. "I lay awake last night, just thinking of you and me, and about what you said yesterday. I'm not above admitting I'm wrong. You were right about handling trouble. Purvane and I will do the rest." She made a wide, inclusive gesture with her right hand. "We're going to be big, Ben. Awfully big. Later we'll need more room, a private office for both of us, but this will do now."

"What would I do with a private office?" He shook his head. "All I need is a jail."

"We don't have one yet, but it's in the plan. I'll show you." She walked quickly to one of the front desks, heels tapping on the plank floor, and, opening a drawer, took out a map. "I'm not fooling myself, Ben. It will be wild around here as long as the construction is going on, but after a year or so it'll quiet down. What I want most of all is to build a town for families."

She sat down and unrolled the map. "This is something else I went ahead on, but if you don't agree, we'll change it." She leaned back in the swivel chair and looked directly at him. "Ben, I've dreamed about this for a long time and that's why I want to do a good job. It's also the reason I've taken so much for granted. I just had a feeling you'd see things the way I do."

He saw that she was not quite sure of herself. He asked, "What things?"

"The things that make us go, I guess." Her blue eyes, always bright, were glowing now with eagerness. "I'm a dreamer. Purvane says that I'm not always practical. Anyhow, what I want to do here is to build a town where people can enjoy living. The irrigation project is something else. Here in town I want a church and a school and a hospital. We owe things like that to the people who will live here just as much as we owe the farmers a ditch that will carry water."

"I hear you talking," he said, "but I still don't savvy."

She laughed softly. "I'm just taking a woman's way to say something. That's always the long way, you know. Let's put it this way. Men are interested in drinking, aren't they? Gambling! Women! I mean men would say that those are things a town should give them."

He nodded. "I guess that's right, but you ain't gonna change men."

"I know that, but what most men forget is that a town also has some women and children. I propose to have two streets so that a good woman can come downtown with her children and not have to pass saloons." She swung back to the desk and tapped the map with her forefinger. "This is Main Street. I thought we'd have the business section here, stores and hotels and all that. Over here is the other street. We might call it River Street. That's where the men can have their fun."

She tilted her head to look up at him, and sat waiting, lips parted. He said, "Lady, I ain't arguing. Sounds like a good idea to me."

"Ben, I . . . think that's wonderful." She took a deep breath. "Last night you were talking about who was to give orders. It's been worrying me ever since." She motioned to the map. "This means a lot to me. I was afraid we just wouldn't agree."

He lifted tobacco and paper from his vest pocket, sensing that there was more to this than she was putting into words. She had gone ahead as if she did not have a partner, confident that she could twist him into her groove of thinking. This was not a question on which he could conscientiously oppose her, yet there was a matter of policy which he could not dodge. If he submitted now, it might be too late when a real question rose between them.

"I ain't bucking you on this," he said, "but I still say that as far as trouble is concerned, I've got to handle it my way." He tapped the star on his shirt. "I took this because you asked me to. Now I've got to handle the job the way I see it."

"Of course, Ben." She rose as if dismissing the matter and motioned toward the next desk. "That's yours. The one behind you is Purvane's. He won't be here much, but I thought he ought to have one."

"I don't need a desk."

"You've got one anyhow. There are times when you'll need to be here. For instance, there's some legal work to be done. We'll have to have an agreement drawn up on both the townsite and the irrigation project."

He shrugged. "I suppose so," he said, irritated a little, for he had never been one to depend on a piece of paper, legal or otherwise. If a man's word wasn't good, some writing on a sheet of paper wouldn't change it.

"I've worked with a lawyer for several years named Lou Fain," she went on. "He's in Salem now ironing out some of the details concerning the segregation. He'll be here the first of the week. He's not like some lawyers. You can trust him." She turned back to the map, lips

pursed as if thinking. "We've got to have a drugstore.
A doctor's office in the back." She tapped the map.
"We'll put it here just west of this building."

A man poked his head through the door. "Sarboe,
you're wanted out here."

Sarboe fired his cigarette, eyes meeting Rita's. He said,
"I'll go see who it is." He lifted his gun and made a quick
check, thinking that Kelly had returned or had sent someone to do his fighting for him. He eased the gun back
into the holster and stepped into the street, then he
stopped, puzzled. It was a woman riding sidesaddle on
a black mare who waited to see him.

Sarboe moved toward her, a hand touching his hat
brim. He said, "I'm Ben Sarboe."

She was silent for a moment, her dark eyes making a
cool study of him. She was a small, slender woman, quite
young, perhaps twenty. Her hair was black, making a
striking contrast with the pale skin of her face. Sarboe's
first thought was that she had come to ask for work and
he doubted that there was any for her. She had the fragile
appearance of one who must be taken care of by others.

"Ben Sarboe," she said in a thoughtful voice. "You
don't look anything like the man I'd pictured. I supposed
you were ten feet tall and fire came out of your nostrils
every time you took a breath."

He laughed. "You sure pegged me wrong, ma'am. I'm
five feet ten, I weigh one hundred and seventy pounds,
and I don't cotton to eating fire."

"I can believe that," she said. "The trouble with Mike
is that his judgment is as variable as the weather. When
he came home last fall he thought you were wonderful.
Now he says you're a crook, a liar, and a cheat."

"I reckon I'm somewhere between." He looked up at
her, wondering. "Mike never said he was married."

She flushed, embarrassed. "I'm sorry. I was so anxious
to see what Ben Sarboe looked like that I forgot you
wouldn't know who I was. I'm Mike's sister Linda."

"Now that I think of it, he did mention a sister, but you sure don't look much like him."

"I know. I don't think or act like he does, either. I suppose we're as far apart as a brother and sister could be, but I love him. That's why I'm here. I don't want him killed, and I don't want to see him hanged for murder."

She had said too much in too short a time for Sarboe to make much sense out of it. He said, "I don't, either."

Rita had come out of the office to stand beside Sarboe. She asked courteously, "Won't you come in?"

"My partner, Miss Gentry." Sarboe motioned toward Rita.

"This is Linda Kelly, Mike's sister."

"How do you do," Linda said. "Thank you, Miss Gentry, but I can't stay. I came to ask Mr. Sarboe to go back with me. Our camp is about four miles down the river."

"He can't go," Rita said sharply. "We're building a town. You can see that for yourself."

Anger stirred in Sarboe. The suspicion that had been in his mind became a certainty. He had made a concession to Rita, but she would be unwilling to make one in return.

"Your town will not suffer for a few hours of Mr. Sarboe's absence," Linda said. "Yesterday he tried to talk to Mike, but Mike wasn't able to talk to him. This morning his temper has cooled off so he can."

"Then let him come here," Rita said.

Linda shook her head. "His pride won't let him. He thinks he's the injured one."

"If he's as intent on making trouble as he was yesterday, it's better that he doesn't show his face around here." Rita turned to the office. "Ben, let's get back to work."

It was a rude dismissal and anger deepened in Sarboe. "It's work you can do without me," he said. "This comes under the heading of trouble. I'll get my horse, Miss Kelly."

Rita gripped his arm, suddenly tense. "You can't go, Ben. You're smart enough to see through this."

His eyes locked with Rita's; his lips were tightly pressed. There were things he wanted to say, things that would have to be said some day, but not before Linda Kelly. He said, "I aimed to hunt Mike up anyhow. You were right yesterday about it being a waste of time to talk to him, but you might be wrong today. I've got to try."

"Then you don't see," Rita breathed. "You don't understand how important you are. They'll kill you."

"There will be no trouble unless Sarboe makes it," Linda said. "I can promise that."

Rita did not look at the other woman. She said, her tone pleading, "Don't go, Ben. I'm asking you not to. Your land is the only good townsite for miles. Kelly knows that and it's the reason he wants it. It's why he was so mad yesterday. He'd have killed you then if he could."

Sarboe had never heard Rita Gentry beg for anything before, not when she had been a girl or since she had come to the Deschutes. He could not doubt the concern that was in her, but he wasn't sure what was the real reason for it.

"I'll get my horse," Sarboe said.

Turning, he strode along the street toward his barn. He did not look back, but he knew she would be staring after him, her eyes hot with rage.

Chapter VII

THE TALK AT DALLAM'S

RITA was not in sight when Sarboe rode out of town with Linda Kelly. Neither spoke for a time. Sarboe stared straight ahead, his thoughts bitter as he asked himself how big a mistake he'd made when he had become Rita's partner. Occasionally Linda glanced at him and then looked away, worry shadowing her thin, pale face.

They were out of the pines and riding through a close-growing forest of juniper when Linda said, "I didn't understand how it was or I wouldn't have come. I want you to believe that."

He gave her a wry grin. "Forget it. Let's say it was a declaration of independence."

"I hope it doesn't make trouble between you. You two are right and Mike's wrong. You see, I think I know George Dallam. That's the reason I came."

He gave her a questioning look. "That needs some explaining."

She shook her head. "Not if you know George Dallam."

"I don't."

She was silent a moment. Then she said, "He's a promoter. When you say that, you say it all. He takes everything he can and gives nothing. I can't prove he's a crook, and I guess no one else can, either, or he'd be in prison."

"Then what's Mike doing with him?"

She frowned, her eyes on the road ahead that ran twisting through the junipers. "There's just Mike and me left of our family. We've never had much money, but Mike's always been ambitious. He's handy with his tongue and he's got a big laugh. You know how it is. He's got a way of making folks like him."

Sarboe nodded. "I know all right. I still like him."

"Well, that answers why Dallam is backing him. Your question has the opposite answer. Mike wants Dallam's money. What he doesn't see is that Dallam will run the business and Mike will have to trail along or get out. Someone may have to take the blame for Dallam's shady tricks and I'm afraid it'll be Mike."

"Nothing I can do about that."

"I'm hoping you can make Mike see this whole thing with a little sense. His trouble is that when he trusts a man, he trusts him completely. That's why he's so mad at you. He just thought you'd go along. He had everything planned including the use of your place for a townsite. Now he's worried Dallam will back out when he finds out what's happened."

They came out of the junipers into an open sage flat scarred by lava outcroppings. Wheel tracks ran westward toward the river, and Linda turned off the road to follow them. Two tents showed above the sage, and Sarboe wondered if this was Kelly's townsite. It was a poor choice. Anyone living here would fry all summer and freeze all winter, for there was nothing to break the wind or give shade. Still, it was probably as good a place as any unless a man went far downstream.

Water was a problem, for the canyon of the Deschutes broke off just beyond the tents. The east wall made a steep slant to the river so that even a narrow, looping road to the bottom would be difficult and expensive to build. It would have to be built if Mike Kelly was to have a town, for there could be no town without water and the Deschutes was the only potential supply.

"The truth is that Mike has more ambition than he has talent or brains," Linda said reluctantly. "He couldn't get anybody but Dallam to back him, so he's talked himself into believing that Dallam's on the level."

They were close to the tents now, and Sarboe could see three horses staked behind them. Linda must have seen them at the same time, for he heard her suck in a quick, scared breath. She said, "Maybe you'd better not go any farther."

"Why?"

"I think Dallam is here. Verd Ricket may be with him. Ricket was waiting for him in The Dalles, but I didn't think they'd be back this soon. I promised there wouldn't be any trouble unless you made it, but I can't keep that promise if Ricket's here."

"We'll play it out," Sarboe said. "I never like to back down when I start a chore."

A moment later they reined up in front of the tents, Linda calling, "Mike."

Kelly pushed the flap back and stepped out, his face holding the marks of Sarboe's fists. He said, his tone friendly enough, "Welcome to Dallamville, Ben."

"Is this the town that's going to be here a hundred years?" Sarboe asked.

"That's right. By that time your Swift River won't be anything but a bad memory. Come in, Ben. I want you to meet George Dallam."

Kelly stepped back into the tent. Sarboe dismounted and followed. A man rose from behind a table and moved around it, soft hand extended. "Sarboe, is it? Well sir, this is a pleasure, a pleasure indeed." He motioned toward a cot. "Sit down, neighbor. We have little to offer in the way of home pleasure, but there will be more, much more. All we need is time."

Sarboe gripped the man's hand and dropped it. He sat down on the cot while Dallam bustled back to his chair behind the table. George Dallam in the flesh broke every preconceived idea that Sarboe had formed of him. A white beard would have made him a perfect candidate to play Santa Claus at a Christmas Eve party. Everything else fitted: sparkling blue eyes that seemed filled with suppressed merriment, pink cheeks, and a round little belly.

Dallam leaned back in his chair. "Well Sarboe, they tell me you had a reputation on the border as a tough lawman. I see you're packing a star. That's good. We need a lawman here on the river." He tapped the table, smiling blandly. "You gave thirty pounds away and licked Mike. If you're as good with a gun as you are with your fists, you'll do, Sarboe, you'll do."

"Aw, he hit me when I wasn't looking," Kelly muttered.

Dallam laughed derisively. "Judging by the appearance of your face, Mike, you must have been looking the other way a good deal of the time."

Kelly remained standing. Linda came in then and Dallam rose. "Ah, Linda, you get prettier every time I see you. You're a lucky man to have such a sister, Mike, very lucky."

Linda said, her voice giving no hint of her feeling, "How are you, George?"

"I'm fine, fine." Dallam unrolled a map, his gaze swinging to Sarboe. "I don't know just why you're here, friend. Mike said Linda had gone after you, but I'm sure you had your own reasons for coming."

"That I did," Sarboe said. "I wanted to talk to Mike. Yesterday he was waiting for me when I got back from Prineville. He was so mad he was crazy. As far as I'm concerned, I don't want trouble. Neither does my partner. I was hoping that Mike wouldn't be so proddy today."

"Nothing's changed," Kelly said sourly. "When a man double-crosses a friend . . ."

"Just a minute, Mike, just a minute." Dallam held up a pudgy hand. "Tell me one thing, Sarboe. How well do you know your partner?"

"Well enough," Sarboe said shortly.

"You realize, of course, that your piece of land is the only place where the Deschutes can be easily forded for a good many miles. You have a meadow which is a natural spot for a town. Therefore your place is very valuable. If you have not signed any papers, I'm prepared to offer you ten thousand dollars for your property."

Sarboe shook his head. "No deal."

"I was afraid that would be your answer." Dallam sighed. "Don't misunderstand me, Sarboe. I do not intend to insult Miss Gentry, although we have had some dealings and I have found her very difficult to do business with. Nor do I intend to infer that she, shall we say, used her female equipment to persuade you to desert Mike . . ."

Sarboe rose. "Dallam, I'm going to . . ."

"No, Ben, no." Linda stepped in front of him. She whispered, "Verd Ricket is in my tent. Don't make trouble."

Sarboe stood motionless, looking down at the girl, his hands fisted at his sides. Rita had been right. It might have been different if he could have talked to Kelly alone, but the way it stood now, there was nothing he could do.

"All right." Sarboe looked past the girl at Dallam. "I hear you've taken Verd Ricket on."

"He's working for us," Dallam said easily. "We needed a man who has lived in this country. We had counted on your doing the job, but when we found you weren't available, we hired Ricket."

"You're in rough company, Mike," Sarboe said.

Sarboe turned and would have walked out if Kelly had not gripped his arm. "Hold on, Ben. I went off half-cocked yesterday. I deserved what I got, so I'm not holding any hard feelings." He held out his hand. "How about it?"

Sarboe grinned as he took Kelly's hand. "Sure, Mike. That's what I came over for. This country's big enough for both of us."

"Perhaps, perhaps," Dallam said. "Come here, will you, Sarboe?"

Kelly motioned toward the table. "Take a look, Ben. He's got something to show you."

Sarboe hesitated, eyes searching Kelly's bruised face that seemed to be innocent of guile. Reluctantly he turned to the table as Dallam placed a finger on a spot near the center of the map.

"Now right here is Dallamville, Sarboe," Dallam said. "In the end we'll be the one to survive just as Mike said. The railroad will decide our fate. That's where my strength lies. You see, I know the railroad powers and I know they will build up the river before long. There is a lesson to be learned from history, my friend. Steel goes where there are people and resources. The resources are waiting on the people and the people will come.''

Dallam's finger moved along the map. ''Here is your town. Now, understand one thing, Sarboe. I doubt that your partner has told you this. Our interest in the Deschutes country has not come as suddenly as you think. The Carey Act has made possible its development. The land is rich, but it needs water, so we'll furnish it, your company and mine. Here is your segregation.'' He made a circle with a fingertip east of the river. He made a second circle north of the first, then tapped a point on the Deschutes three miles above Swift River. ''Both of our ditches will have to come out here. Geography dictates these things, Sarboe.''

Dallam leaned back, smiling blandly. Sarboe said impatiently, ''Well?''

''I have a proposition. Interested?''

''No.''

''Don't jump so fast, my friend. I realize that Miss Gentry is brilliant and strong-minded as well as beautiful. Personally, I don't approve of women mixing in business any more than I approve of them getting the vote. Why, the first thing we know they'll be wanting to hold office.''

''I'm listening,'' Sarboe said.

''Ah, that's better, that's better. If you are a partner, you will have as much to say about your company's policies as Miss Gentry. That's why I was glad to see you ride in today. Now here is my proposition. As you say, the country is big enough for both of us. Before fall comes, I have no doubt there will be enough people here to settle both of our segregations.''

Sarboe threw up his hands. ''Oh hell, you keep talking, but you don't say nothing.''

''He's that way,'' Linda said.

Irritation stirred in Dallam's eyes. He said softly, "Now Linda, now Linda." He pinned his gaze on Sarboe's face again. "One ditch will do for both of us. That's my offer, neighbor. It will save money for us and it will result in considerable saving to the settlers."

Sarboe stared at the man. On the face of it Dallam's proposal seemed logical. If it had been any other man, Sarboe would have said yes, but he had no reason to trust Dallam and he knew exactly what Rita would say.

Sarboe shook his head. "No."

Kelly swore. "You damned cheating son! I told George that was what you'd say. That woman of yours listened to everything I had to say and then . . ."

"Shut up, Mike," Linda said sharply. "You always did talk too much."

"Maybe so, but what kind of a person would take another man's idea and then rush in ahead of him? I tell you I'll bust you, Sarboe. Before we're done . . ."

"Mike!" Linda shook his arm. "Stop that. Ben never made you a promise of any kind."

"Very true, very true," Dallam said smoothly. "I had hoped we could come to a peaceful settlement that would prevent trouble, but I see that it is impossible. We'll build our town, Sarboe. We'll last and you'll go bust. What's more, I think our proposition will appeal to the settlers where yours never will."

Sarboe had moved to the tent opening. He said, "If you want a fight, you'll get one. Go ahead with your town and ditch. We'll see to ours."

"But there is need for only one town," Dallam said, "and in the long run there will be as much profit in developing a townsite as there is in putting water on the land. That means one of us will fail and one will succeed."

"And we'll be the one to succeed," Kelly shouted. "I don't give a damn about the rules, Ben. We aim to win."

"You ever figure out where you'll wind up?" Sarboe asked.

"You bet I have. They'll be writing a history of Oregon about 1950 and there'll be a hell of a good chapter about Mike Kelly and George Dallam, but nary a word about Ben Sarboe."

"Quite true, quite true," Dallam said, pleased.

"We'll see," Sarboe said, and left the tent.

Verd Ricket was not in sight. Sarboe stepped in the saddle, unaware that Linda had followed until she said, "I'm sorry, Ben. It was a waste of time just as Miss Gentry said."

"Not exactly. I learned something." He sat in his saddle, looking down at the girl's troubled face. Then he asked, "How come you're here?"

"I'm supposed to be a secretary," she said wryly, "but so far there hasn't been anything for me to do. I guess it was a bad bargain all around."

"If it turns out so bad you can't stand it, you'll be welcome in Swift River."

"I'll remember," she said, "but I hope it won't come to that."

He touched the brim of his hat and reined around. This visit had not been a waste of time, he thought, as he rode back to Swift River, not at all. He understood Mike Kelly now as he had not understood him before. Linda had pegged her brother when she'd told Sarboe that Mike had more ambition than talent. Too, Sarboe had met Dallam and that was well worth the time he had invested.

Sarboe expected to hear some bitter words from Rita when he got back, but there were none. She came out of the cabin as he was putting his horse away, her face composed.

"I have your dinner ready, Ben," she said.

"That's good news," he said, and told her about Dallam's offer.

"You did exactly right," she said gravely. "I would never under any circumstances make a deal with George Dallam."

He walked back to the cabin with Rita, thankful that he was not getting the tongue lashing he had expected, but he knew that nothing had been settled between them.

Chapter VIII

TOWN MEETING

SARBOE had never witnessed the birth of a town before, and it was unlikely he would ever see anything like it again. During May Swift River became a town. Every day the lava dust was stirred into a gray haze by wagons hauling lumber and hay from Prineville; other wagons freighted supplies in from Shaniko that had come by rail. Each southbound stage was loaded to capacity, and the driver, Barney Johns, shook his head and swore he couldn't believe what he was seeing.

Word had fanned out all over the state that life was exploding here on the Deschutes. There was the riffraff that Sarboe had expected, but there were others, too: laborers, teamsters, carpenters, men who honestly wanted work. They found it here. Most of them came alone, but a few brought their families and set up tents among the stumps at the edge of the clearing.

Work was started on the ditch. Heavy machinery for a sawmill was laboriously hauled south from Shaniko and set up beside the river. Four times a day its whistle shrilled into the mountain silence, setting the pattern of life with clock-like accuracy. Every daylight hour was filled with the clamor of saw and hammer, and Main Street became a canyon flanked by false fronts of new pine lumber.

Through all the activity the Deschutes rolled northward unchanged, disdaining the puny efforts of man to change this country that had so long gone unchanged, intent only on reaching its destination.

Sarboe had thought he would have nothing to do; he had supposed when Rita had first talked him into the partnership that he would be a mere spectator to this business of rolling back the wilderness. It was not that way. He had never been busier in his life.

Once he accompanied the sheriff into the lava country southeast of Swift River after a horse thief. They found their man and brought him back. He patrolled the town on Saturday nights and occasionally had to throw a drunk into the little log jail, but usually a word was enough to restore order. There was something about Ben Sarboe that discouraged most men from asking for trouble.

Handling the mail was a job by itself. More coaches had been put on the run between Shaniko and Swift River so that now there was a stage every day, each bringing a heavier load of mail. Sarboe made another rack to hang on his wall, then a third. He thought with a trace of sourness that his life was being changed more rapidly than the country.

His old friends dropped in for the mail, but now there was no time to sit and talk or ask them to stay for a meal. When he wasn't busy with the mail, he was working with the cattle that had been driven in from Prineville or helping butcher or going after more. As Rita said, men worked better when they were fed well, and beef for the tent dining table was her major extravagance.

Sarboe did not see any of the Rickets until late in the month when Holt rode in for the mail. There was only a catalog for them, and Holt seemed relieved when he asked, "That all?" and Sarboe nodded.

Holt sat his saddle for a moment, staring along the street, a dark and slender man who was afraid. He was as different from Verd as two men could be, and Sarboe wondered about it just as he often wondered about the mail that the Rickets came for and seldom received. What they did get was usually nothing more than an advertisement of some sort or a catalog, yet they had always seemed to expect something.

Holt brought his gaze to Sarboe. "Making a lot of money, ain't you?"

"Haven't seen any of it yet."

"Funny what a man will do for money," Holt said somberly. "Why couldn't you just let things alone?"

Irritated, Sarboe said, "I didn't turn this loose." He motioned toward the Deschutes. "I couldn't stop it no more than I could stop that river from flowing."

"Ain't gonna bother us," Holt said as if he hoped it wouldn't. "Seen Verd lately?"

"No."

Holt shifted the catalog to his other hand. "Don't make me and Dad no never mind what happens to you, but Dad don't want Verd to get into no trouble. You watch out for him. He ain't gonna rest till he gets you."

"I hear he's thrown in with Dallam and Kelly."

"So he said. Well, the pay's good and he wants to be on the other side so he'll have a good reason to whittle you down. He don't need no reason, though. He'll whittle you down anyhow if you don't get out of the country."

Sarboe studied young Ricket, wondering why he felt that Verd needed a defense. Sarboe said, "Maybe Verd figures Dallam is big enough to protect him."

"He's big enough he don't need protection from a hairpin like George Dallam," Holt said, and rode away.

Sarboe watched him until he disappeared in the pines. What Holt had said didn't seem to make much sense. Perhaps Verd wanted the good pay. Or, and this seemed more likely, Verd saw a fight shaping up and wanted a part of it. Whatever motive was behind Verd's action in going over to Dallam, Sarboe had a feeling that neither Cap nor Holt approved.

A snowstorm struck early in May, leaving a foot of wet snow. It brought some suffering to the women and children huddled in tents and covered wagons, and it gave Rita more worry than Sarboe had expected. It was another facet of her character that he had not seen before, and he liked her the better for it. Book work had piled up, but she took time to see that all the children had warm clothes. If the men were short of money, she gave them an advance, or told the storekeeper, Abe Tottle, to give them credit.

Sarboe found little time to talk with Rita these days. They were like two feathers caught in the whirlwind. There was too much to be done in a short time. They took their meals in the dining tent, but they seldom ate at the same time. Usually when Sarboe went to bed in the barn, the windows of his cabin were dark, but there would be a light in the townsite office.

It was on a Sunday in the middle of May when Rita unexpectedly asked Sarboe and Purvane to have dinner with her. It was the first meal she had cooked since the day Sarboe had returned from his talk with Dallam and Kelly. There had been no clash between her and Sarboe since then, a fact which proved nothing. There had not been anything to clash over, but Sarboe was never entirely free from the fear that it had to come and he hated the thought.

Sarboe's own feelings were not clear to him. He had loved Rita as a girl. There was no reason he should not love her now, no reason except that she was like a ship bound for a certain port, and nothing would keep her from reaching it. He kept telling himself that he did not love her now; it had just been a feeling any kid would have for a girl who appealed to him. Love, he kept telling himself, was a thing which must be returned in kind.

Rita had said he was to forget she was a woman. He was convinced now she had meant it. She needed him just as she needed Fred Purvane and the newspaper man, John Meacham, and the storekeeper, Abe Tottle. That wasn't good enough for Ben Sarboe, so he bottled up his feelings.

He told himself that when this was finished, he'd drift on just as he had drifted before he had come to the Deschutes. Not that this wasn't a job worth doing. It was, and he realized that his own ideas on the matter had changed, but he simply couldn't go on living here, seeing Rita every day and smothering his feelings for her so that it would not leap into flame.

Eventually his thoughts made a complete circle and brought him to the inescapable conclusion that there would never be another woman for him. Some day she might meet a man who could reach behind her pride and her ambition and touch her heart. Sarboe had lost hope that it would ever be he.

It was a warm Sunday, warm enough to give hope that spring had finally come to the Deschutes, warm enough to sit by the open door and smoke while Rita finished dinner. Watching her, Sarboe felt the old hunger for her. It was, he thought, a mistake to come.

Rita had been careless with her hair and her clothes through these hectic weeks when she seemed to run from one task to another. She wasn't careless today. That was one of the things which puzzled him about her. She could be brisk and efficient and business-like day after day, her smiles perfunctory, her glances impersonal. Today she was utterly different.

Her hair had been brushed until it was brilliant amber; her eyes held that bright eagerness for living he had noticed when she had first come to the river. She was wearing a blue dress that made a perfect fit over breasts and hips, the sort of dress that a woman would wear for a particular man.

Hope stirred briefly in Sarboe as he thought of that, then he pushed it out of his mind. Probably spring had touched her, not any deep personal interest in Ben Sarboe. Tomorrow she would put on her rumpled brown suit again and get back to the job of empire building.

She set a platter of steak on the table, frowning. "I told Fred to be here at two . . ."

"He's coming."

"Well, it's time." She gave Sarboe a quick smile. "Holler at him to hurry, Ben."

Sarboe rose and tossed a cigarette into the grass. "Get a move on, Fred. Rita says she's about to throw it out."

"I'm coming," Purvane shouted, "and I'm empty all the way down. Don't let her do nothing foolish."

He came in, a lantern-jawed, harried man. The lines around his pale blue eyes seemed deeper than usual, and Sarboe, looking at him as he stepped through the door, wondered if the man ever rested.

Rita must have had the same thought, for she said, "You look tired, Fred."

"I am. Next fall I'm gonna find me a hole and sleep all winter."

"Trouble?" Rita asked.

"A little. I've never been up against so much rock work, and I ain't real sure the ditch will hold water when we get it done."

Sarboe asked, "Why?"

Purvane grimaced. "It's this damned lava. Cracks to hellangone when you blow a piece out. We may have to flume all of it."

"That'll cost money," Sarboe said.

"Plenty," Purvane agreed. "Well, we'll see. Oughta be some way to fill them cracks."

"Let's sit down before we spoil our appetite worrying about it," Rita said.

Worry spoiled no appetite that day. Sarboe had never eaten so much before in his life. Rita brought a peach pie to the table when they were ready for it and cut it into quarters, glancing at Sarboe apologetically.

"Don't make any remarks about how much I've eaten today," she said. "I didn't have any breakfast. I slept the clock around. Better try it, Fred."

"I aim to, come fall," he told her.

Nothing more was said about the cost of the ditch, but Sarboe wondered about it. Rita had never indicated how much money she was willing to put into the project, or how much she had. Since Sarboe had nothing to contribute, it was not a question he could very well ask, but when he had finished his pie and shaken his head at the remaining piece, he asked, "Why can't you sell stock?"

"I'll go broke first," Rita said quickly. "I've seen too many mines financed that way, all on the basis of fine promises, then the company goes broke when the vein pinches out. The suckers wind up with nothing but tons of country rock."

"I talked to Kelly yesterday," Purvane said. "They're starting work on their ditch in the morning. He said Dallam had sold enough stock to get under way."

"That's like Dallam." Rita rose. "Let's get over to the office. We're organizing a commercial club this afternoon."

"Ah hell!" Purvane yawned. "This is Sunday."

"This is a Sunday job," Rita said.

They left the cabin, Rita between the two men. Some boys were fishing and Sarboe turned his head to watch. He dropped behind, then hurried to catch up. "Sure getting back on my fishing," he said. "I was figuring that this afternoon we could . . ."

"Later," Rita said impatiently, "if there's time."

They walked on in silence, Rita staring ahead, a frown cutting across her forehead. She was planning the meeting, Sarboe thought, and it struck him that her very strength and intentness of purpose was her weakness. She could not relax once this thing was under way. He knew that only the weight of sheer weariness had forced her to sleep the clock around last night. Now, on Sunday, when she should be going fishing she was organizing a commercial club.

The others were in the townsite office when Rita stepped through the door, Purvane and Sarboe following. With the exception of Doc Zachary, they were men Rita had worked with before, and they had followed her here because they believed in her and the future of this country.

Sarboe nodded at them and sat down at his desk, the first time he had sat here in more than a week. He leaned back in the swivel chair and rolled a smoke, wondering how many of these men would stay when the hurly-burly of starting a new project was over. He had asked himself the same question about Rita. He wasn't sure that any of them had the capacity to sink their roots and help nourish a new country through the hard years that always follow the first burst of activity, or whether they only wanted the big profits that accompany a boom and would drift on in a few months like fiddle-footed cowhands intent only on seeing over the next hill.

Firing his cigarette, Sarboe flipped the match through the open door, irritation stirring in him. He had no right to mentally criticize any of them. Maybe they were drifters, but he was no better. Not once had he put his shoulder to the wheel and helped make the long pull that follows the first flush of prosperity when a new country is opened up.

There were five men in the room. John Meacham, editor of the *Swift River Clarion*, was a tall man with red-veined eyes and ink-stained fingers who had already printed his first issue that had glowed with bright promises about a potential Garden of Eden on the banks of the Deschutes. Abe Tottle who operated both the store and hotel was there, Lou Fain the lawyer, Doc Zachary, and the banker, Otis Barrett.

Good men, Sarboe thought, honest and loyal and convinced that everything Meacham had said in the *Clarion* was true. But hopes for tomorrow are one thing, facts of today are another. The tenacity of their faith was still untested.

Rita sat down on top of her desk. The men were scattered around the room, smoking and talking. Now they swung to face her and were suddenly silent. It was probably old and familiar business to all of them except Doc Zachary, Sarboe thought, and he doubted that there was one in the bunch who would question anything Rita said.

"You did a good job, John." Rita nodded at Meacham. "Get the *Clarion* into people's hands and they'll come."

Pleased, Meacham said, "There are other ways, too, Rita. I'm getting stories out to the papers in The Dalles, Portland, Salem, Albany, and Boise. It will take a little time, but I think that by the first of July we'll see settlers coming in. Next spring we'll witness a veritable land rush from the Middle West."

Barrett took his cigar out of his mouth and leaned forward. He was a little sharp-eyed man close to fifty with thin sandy hair that was brushed across his head in a manner that made the most of what he had. He said, "Rita, I think John should bear down on one thing. In a homestead country we often get a raggle-taggle type of settler who expects free land. This country needs solid farmers prepared to pay their way. If the *Clarion* tells them that, we'll weed out the failures at the start."

Rita nodded. "Good idea, Otis."

Abe Tottle lifted his feet to his desk. He said, "It'll take money to stay at my hotel. It'll take money to buy grub at my store. I don't aim to give credit till I know who's good, and you can't tell that in a year. Takes time."

"I don't think we need to be alarmed about our type of settlers," Rita said. "Right now our job is advertising what we're doing and what we have to offer. That's why we need a Commercial Club. For the first year or more the paper will have to be subsidized and the company can't do it all."

Lou Fain nodded. He was a fat man, too fat for his thirty-five years. Any mild exercise started him wheezing, a weakness which he blamed on the altitude. He said in his slow way, "We understand that, Rita. We're all making money but John, and he won't make anything until there are enough people here to support a newspaper, but the question is, how deep are we going to dig into our pockets?"

"I suggest one hundred dollars apiece," Rita said. "That makes three hundred for the company." She nodded toward Sarboe and Purvane. "Eight hundred for all of us. John will pay with the rest. As other businessmen come in, I'll see that they throw into the kitty. John can draw on the fund as he needs it."

They nodded agreement as Sarboe knew they would. Rita had planned everything, even to having Meacham prepared with a constitution ready to be read. It was promptly accepted and signed. Otis Barrett was elected President, Fain Vice-President, and Meacham Secretary-Treasurer. Sarboe sat motionless, watching and listening, a little amused at the way Rita had rigged it down to the last detail.

When the business was finished, Rita said, "The company has sold some lots but we've got to do better. The townsite has to keep us solvent until the ditch is a paying proposition." She motioned toward Purvane. "Fred tells me the construction will be more expensive than he had originally thought, so we may be strained a little."

"We're all in this," Barrett said. "It's a poor kind of bank that won't stand behind its community."

"Thank you, Otis," Rita said softly. "Ben and I appreciate that, but we won't call for help unless we have to. Fred was saying that Dallam has sold stock in his company, but as far as I'm concerned, I aim to take the risks." She slid off the desk, smiling a little. "I guess that winds things up for today. Our next job is to organize our town. We need a council and mayor and marshal. Ben is a deputy sheriff, but it would be a good idea to appoint him marshal, too. The company went ahead and built a jail. We expect to be paid back for that.''

"Sure," Doc Zachary said, "and we need a school-house, but what I'm wondering about is a hospital.''

"We can't bite off too much," Barrett said, suddenly cautious.

Zachary was the youngest of the lot, somewhere in his middle twenties and not long out of medical school, Sarboe guessed. He was a big man with a youthful, muscle-ridged face and an easy smile. So far there had been little for him to do, and Sarboe, who had watched him romp with the boys, was reminded of an overgrown Labrador puppy every time he saw the man. But now Zachary was frowning, not satisfied to drop the matter here.

"It's been a mighty healthy community so far," Zachary said, "but when the hot weather gets here there'll be more people and more health problems. Might have a typhoid epidemic. I tell you we've got to be ready for it.''

From the way Rita stood biting her lower lip, Sarboe judged that this was something she had not been prepared for. She said then, rather sharply, "Doctor, you're the only one here except Ben who has not worked with me before. The rest of them know, and I want you to know, that human life and welfare is more important to me than any profit I'll ever make, but we can't extend ourselves too far. The hospital will have to wait.''

Zachary looked down at the floor, big face showing he was unconvinced, but he let it go at that. Sarboe felt a sudden glow of satisfaction. Rita needed opposition and Doc Zachary would give it to her.

"That ends the business . . ." Rita began.

"I've got something to say," Sarboe broke in.

It was the first word he had said since he had come

in. Their eyes turned to him. He saw that they were surprised, and he felt for tobacco and paper, his gaze dropping. Rita had shown she expected him to be a silent partner. Obviously, the rest expected the same.

"Go ahead," Rita said.

Sarboe dribbled tobacco into the paper. "Strikes me that everybody has been overlooking one thing."

There was a moment of silence while he sealed his cigarette and slid it into his mouth. Then Lou Fain asked, "What?"

"Fun," Sarboe answered.

There was another moment of silence and a tension that had been entirely absent crept into the room. Then Rita laughed softly. She said, "Fishing, I suppose?"

"That's right," Sarboe said. "Look at you, working so hard you're all in. Purvane, too. Talking about sleeping all winter. I haven't talked to Doc, but I've got a hunch he'll agree that playing is just as important as working."

"Sure," Zachary said. "All work and no play . . ."

"I know," Rita broke in, "but we've got more work to do . . ."

"Wait a minute," Sarboe said mildly. "I've got an idea for Meacham. He wants to boost Swift River. Now I don't care how much money a man wants to make or how good a home he wants for his family. He'll still want some fun. Well, the Fourth of July is coming along. Why not put on a shindig that'll give Meacham something to write about?"

"I understand that Prineville is putting on a celebration," Meacham objected. "I doubt that we'd have much of a crowd."

"What sort of doings?" Sarboe asked.

Meacham shrugged. "Oh, the usual ball game and band concert and fireworks."

"Then make this different," Sarboe said. "We can have folks coming from Portland and Salem and The Dalles. Might even get the governor if we play it up big."

"How different?" Lou Fain asked skeptically.

"Big different. Something folks never heard about before."

"Got an idea?" Fain pressed.

Sarboe nodded. "A trout barbecue."

"Fish," Rita cried. "Can't you think of anything but fish?"

"It'd be different," Sarboe said.

Again there was silence, Rita frowning as she considered this. It was Purvane who said thoughtfully, "It's a damned good idea, Rita. The men would have something to look forward to."

"And me something to write about," Meacham added. "Let's do it."

"Who's going to bring in the trout?" Fain demanded.

"I will with some help," Sarboe said. "How about you going with me?"

"Me?" Fain looked shocked. "I couldn't stand a fishing trip. The altitude . . ."

"I'll go," Zachary said.

"It's a deal if the fish will oblige," Sarboe said. "For them that don't like fish we'll have bear steak. You bring the bear in, Lou."

They laughed, all but Fain who grunted, "I think I'll be busy."

"Then it's settled," Rita said. "Otis, you go ahead with the plans. John, write it big. If there is anything Ben knows, it's fish."

"Nothing under a foot long," Sarboe said. "You'll have trout running out of your ears."

They broke up then, Sarboe lingering until Rita was ready to lock up. She put her hands on her hips, smiling at him as she said, "Old man of the mountains! Aren't you ever going to think of anything but fish?"

He laughed. "Not if I can help it." He sobered then. "I'd like to know what happened to you. We used to go fishing together and you had a lot of fun."

She turned toward the door, her face grave as if she were touched by old and poignant memories. "I was pretty shallow-headed then, Ben. I had time for fun. I don't now."

He followed her into the street. "You just think you don't. Let's go get my pole. I'll let you catch every other one."

"I meant what I said, Ben. I don't have time . . ." She stopped, breathing hard. Then she asked bitterly, "What's she doing here?"

Startled, he looked up the street, finding it hard to believe what he saw. Linda Kelly had just ridden out of the pines and was coming toward them. Then he remembered he had told her to come to Swift River if Dallamville got too rough for her, but he had not supposed she would.

Chapter IX

REFUGE

LINDA KELLY had felt a responsibility for Mike as far back as she could remember. It was a strange thing which she had never understood, for Mike was four years older and should have looked out for her, but it had not worked that way. Actually those four years meant nothing.

In many ways Linda had been grown up at ten, but Mike wasn't grown up yet and she doubted if he ever would be. If a man who was twenty-five still viewed life with the dreamy eyes of a wishful adolescent, the chances were he would go through the rest of his years refusing to come to grips with reality.

After Sarboe's visit Dallam had returned to Portland and Mike was gone more days than he was in his tent. Verd Ricket had disappeared. So Linda had little to do but idle away her time. She was drawing a salary as secretary of the Dallam-Kelly Development Company, or so George Dallam had told her before he'd left, and there would be plenty for her to do when work was started on the ditch. Meanwhile she could have a vacation on pay.

But the discontent in her grew, for she was not one to enjoy idleness and this was the last place in Oregon she would have picked to spend a vacation. At first she had been able to sit for an hour at a time and look at the long skyline of the Cascades, but there came a day when the scenery bored her.

Cooking was a problem, for Mike often forgot to cut wood for her, and working her way down the side of the canyon and climbing back with buckets of water was sheer labor that filled her with crushing weariness. Yet she was glad of it. At least she could sleep at night, a few hours out of every twenty-four when her mind was not buzzing with a thousand worry devils.

It would have helped if she'd had some sewing or embroidery. A decent stove to cook on. Books to read. But there was nothing, and she hated the things that necessity forced upon her. Like finding a dead juniper and cutting it for wood. Her hands were more calloused than Mike's. The dry wind and the harsh Central Oregon sun roughened the skin of her face and gave her a tan she had never known in the Willamette Valley.

She might as well be a homesteader's wife, she thought rebelliously. At least she would be working for someone she loved while here she was tacitly agreeing to a bargain that would eventually disgrace her brother. There were times when she could have killed George Dallam. But she would only have made Mike hate her if she had.

Once when Mike told her that Dallam was selling shares of stock to raise money to start construction, she tried to talk to him, to say that Dallam was a crook or he'd be using his own money. She accomplished nothing except to send Mike into a towering rage. He shouted that it was a chance of a lifetime, that Dallam was putting up some of his own money and if he, Mike, had enough capital to match Dallam's, no stock would be sold.

When Mike asked her what proof she had that Dallam wasn't on the level, she had to admit she had none. It was just a feeling, a woman's intuition, she said. He was too smooth, too soft, too pious. So Mike plunged into another ranting lecture, shouting that she had to have better grounds than a woman's intuition to condemn Dallam, that he was sound or he'd never have been given the segregation, and she had better be loyal to the company she worked for. Mike wound up by accusing her of being in love with Sarboe.

Linda dropped the matter then. It was one thing she did not want to discuss. After she went to bed she stared up at the tent top, wondering. She had never been in love. Somehow Mike had filled her mind and heart. From the time he had been a boy he had talked big, telling her that the world was his oyster and he'd have it open before he was thirty.

For a long time she had believed him and she had encouraged him, following him from one job to another. Finally she had recognized the truth. It was exactly as she had told Sarboe. Mike had more ambition than talent. Actually it was worse than that. He was lazy. Whenever he was fired, and that was often, someone else had been to blame, never Mike Kelly.

She saw it with stark clarity, here in the darkness and stillness of the night. She got up and, slipping into her robe, stepped out of the tent and looked up at the wind-polished stars that seemed so close here in this thin clean air. Somewhere up there among those stars there must be a God who knew what was coming and would prevent it. Mike wasn't bad; he deserved saving. She breathed a prayer for him, not a very coherent one, but it was a prayer.

When she went back to bed she thought about Ben Sarboe and wondered if she was in love with him as Mike had said. No, it was ridiculous. She couldn't be. Why, she'd been with him only part of one day. Love took more time than that. Besides, she couldn't love a man who didn't love her and she had no reason to think he did. Probably he was in love with Rita Gentry whether he knew it or not.

Still, her thoughts brought her nothing but a vague uneasiness. No amount of reasoning could prove that she wasn't in love. A woman simply didn't reason herself in or out of love. She had been drawn to Sarboe. There was no honest denial of that in her mind.

Thinking about him now, she wondered what there was about him that attracted her. She had sensed a great strength in him. Perhaps that was it, for Sarboe seemed to have an inner toughness that she admired. There was something else, too, that balanced his toughness. Honesty. Or an instinctive goodness, although goodness was not a word that seemed to fit Sarboe.

She wondered if he was happy and decided he wasn't. She had a feeling that he was pursuing something he didn't quite understand, or perhaps he was being torn between two things he wanted. Whatever it was, she was certain he was not a man to chase anything as wispy as the dreams that filled Mike's head. When she slept at last, she was still as unsure of her feelings as when she had gone to bed, but it had been pleasant, thinking about Ben Sarboe.

Even though Mike knew that Linda was not with him in spirit, he could not help bragging to her. He was getting things lined up, he said. He spent most of his time in Prineville arranging for hay, lumber, and steers to feed the men. By the middle of May men and teams would be rolling in. The ditch was the big thing, not the townsite. Perhaps the railroad would come, but there was still no tangible evidence of its coming, and Linda suspected that Dallam would not push his town until he had such evidence.

Dallam and Verd Ricket rode into camp on a Saturday. The snowstorm had delayed them, Dallam said, and it had delayed his men and horses, but they were on the way. Work would start on Monday. Early Sunday morning Mike left for Prineville, and that afternoon the thing finally happened which Linda had expected. She had not known what it would be or when it would come; she had simply been certain in her mind that sooner or later she would have to leave.

There had been a good deal of activity on the sage flat all day. Wagons had begun rolling in Saturday afternoon. Now there was a flurry of getting ready: mending harness, shoeing horses, greasing wagons. They'd pull out for the river above Sarboe's town at dawn Monday. A maddening sense of worry had been tugging at Linda's nerves all day. It wasn't based on anything definite; it was simply that when the work actually started Mike would go on through to the finish. She had never given up the hope that she could get Mike to pull out before this day came.

Acting on sudden impulse, Linda left her tent to talk to Dallam. She wasn't sure in her own mind what she would say. She had thought of asking him what she was supposed to do. She had been paid the evening before, fifty dollars for a month's work she had not done.

Well, she wouldn't sit here twiddling her thumbs through the rest of May. If Dallam thought he could buy her support by paying her for work that was not here to be done he was wrong. There was something else and it would be hard to ask, but she had to know what Dallam planned and how Mike fitted into the picture.

But Linda never asked the questions she wanted to ask. The flap of Mike's tent was down, and she heard Dallam say in a cold calculating voice that was not at all like his usual velvet-smooth tone, "The Gentry woman got herself a trump card when she nailed Sarboe. He's the sort who'll use his gun and spurs on anybody that gets in their way."

"Hell, we can give 'em back as good as they send," Verd said. "This job is gonna be more fun than anything I ever done."

"You sure Purvane don't know you?"

"Sure I'm sure."

"Then start riding. Be on hand first thing in the morning. Stay out of Sarboe's way till the sign's right."

"I know what to do," Verd said irritably.

Linda stepped back from the tent, her heart hammering. She didn't know what they planned, but obviously Dallam thought Mike wouldn't like it, or he wouldn't have waited until Mike was gone to send Verd Ricket on his way.

Verd came out of the tent, saw Linda, and paused. She hated him and she was afraid of him, but she stood her ground, eyes meeting his. She had never seen an uglier face nor one that was filled with more wickedness. He rolled a smoke, taking his time as his dark eyes moved down her slender body, paused on the curve of hip and thigh, and then briefly touched her ankles.

"You're purtier than when you came," Verd said, gaze lifting to her face. "Getting a little color in your cheeks. When I first saw you, you looked like a potato sprout in a cellar."

"Thanks, if that's a compliment," she said, and turned toward her tent.

"Hold on." He caught up with her and, gripping her arm, turned her to face him, brown lips trembling. "You ain't got no call to act high and mighty just because you're Mike Kelly's sister. Before we're done that windbag brother of yours is gonna need me."

She tried to break loose and could not. She whispered, "Let go or I'll call Dallam. I'll tell Mike . . ."

He let her go, snickering. "Sure scares me when you talk about telling Mike. I'll be gone for a day or so, but when I get back, it'd be a damned good idea for Mike if you try being friendly."

Wheeling away from her, he moved across the flat toward his horse, a square-bodied bull of a man who could have torn her arm out of its socket. For a moment panic threatened to sweep through her. She was frightened, more frightened than she had ever been of a man in her life. She couldn't stay. She couldn't tell Mike because it would only turn Verd against him. But regardless of Mike, she spent too many hours here alone to risk being caught by Ricket.

Quickly Linda whirled and ran to her tent. She picked up a few things she would need and stuffed them into a sack. The only money she had was the fifty dollars Dallam had given her. Her mind reached out into the hours ahead. Prineville was a long ways off and she didn't know how to get there. Swift River was the only place she could go to. Sarboe had told her to come if she couldn't stay here.

When she left the tent she saw that Verd Ricket had gone. For a moment she thought of leaving a note for Mike and decided against it. If she was going to make a break with him, it must be clean and final. She wasn't sure he would care, one way or the other. At the moment she thought she hated him for bringing her here. But it was like him. He had not given her a thought; he had little capacity for thinking of anything or anybody but himself. Well, he could go on thinking about himself. She had given too much and received too little. This was something she should have done a long time ago.

She saddled her mare, tied the sack on behind, and stepped up. Then she heard Dallam's soft voice, "Taking a ride?"

Startled, she turned her head, hoping he would not sense the panic that threatened her. She said, "I thought I would."

He stood with his back against the canvas of her tent, smiling genially, soft hands folded across the bulge of his belly. He had never, she thought, looked as much like an innocent little fat man as he did now.

"I have some work for you to do tomorrow," Dallam said. "I'm leaving in the morning, so I thought I'd line you out on it this afternoon."

Panic crowded her then. She would not be stopped now. She cried out, "You can go to hell. I'm quitting."

Her words slapped the smile off his face. He moved toward her, saying, "Get off that horse. I don't aim for Sarboe to get his hands on you."

"I can't stay here. Not with Verd Ricket around."

"I said to get off that horse."

She had never seen a gun on him, but she had often noticed the bulge under his left armpit. Now his right hand was moving toward it. She slapped her mare with the reins and dug in her heels, sending the mare plunging toward Dallam. He jumped sideways and fell and crawled on his hands and knees like a fat, frantic bug.

Linda did not know how close her mare's hoofs had come to Dallam and she didn't care. She went across the flat in a hard run, dust whirling behind her, raced on past the teamsters who turned to look at her, and then she was in the junipers. She pulled her mare down and looked back, wondering if Dallam would send someone after her, but there was no pursuit. Apparently he was willing to let her go.

She rode on, slowly, and suddenly she began to tremble. Dallam had never treated her that way before; she had never seen him make a motion toward his gun before. She wondered how near death she had been. It was something she would never know, but she had found out one thing. She had long been suspicious of George Dallam, but she had still taken him too lightly.

By the time Linda reached Swift River, she had regained control of her emotions. She was stunned by the amount of work that had been done since she had been here a month before. Then she saw Sarboe and Rita on the walk in the middle of the block and she rode toward them, wondering how she could say what she had to say.

Sarboe stepped into the street, touching the brim of his hat to her. He said, "Howdy. Ride over to take a look at Swift River?"

Linda threw a quick glance at Rita who remained on the walk. She saw no welcome on the other woman's face. A crushing sense of inadequacy filled Linda. It was the first time she had ever seen a woman who seemed completely self-possessed and certain of her destiny. If Rita had been in her shoes, she would have stayed in Dallamville and handled the situation. She had the look of a person who could meet any crisis that came to her.

"I didn't come just to look." Linda's gaze was on Sarboe's face, searching for some sign that she was not welcome, but there was none. "I came to stay."

"Now that's something." Rita stepped off the walk and moved to stand beside Sarboe. "Dallam sent you to spy on us. That it?"

"No. I couldn't stay there any longer and I don't have any other place to go." Linda gripped the saddle horn, swaying a little, dark eyes begging Sarboe. "If you think I came to spy . . ."

"I don't think anything of the kind," Sarboe broke in, "but I'm wondering why you'd pull out on Mike?"

"I can't do him any good," she said miserably. She told them about Verd Ricket and Dallam, adding, "I thought I could find work here. I'll do . . . anything."

"Anything?" Rita's brows lifted.

"Anything that's decent. There must be work in a new town."

"Not for you," Rita said quickly. "What work we have we'll give to the wives of our men."

Sarboe scratched a cheek, puzzled eyes on Rita. "That don't sound like you. Sometimes you've got a heart as big as a house, but right now I'd say it was the size of a mustard seed."

Rita put her hands on her hips, eyes scornful. "You're such a fool, Ben. Or maybe it takes another woman to see through her. She'd never leave her brother. Dallam wants to find out what's going on, and this is a smart way of doing the job."

"If you think I'm a liar, you'll have to go on thinking it," Linda cried. "If you'll tell me how to get to Prineville . . ."

"You're staying here." Sarboe's tone was sharply final. "You couldn't get to Prineville before dark."

"There's no place for her to stay," Rita said evenly. "The hotel won't be open for a couple of days yet . . ."

"I've got a cabin," Sarboe said. "Remember?"

The color deepened in Rita's cheeks, but her mouth was smiling. "I'm not likely to forget, but let's be practical, Ben. I'm moving to the hotel as soon as my room's ready. Then what will she do?"

"She can stay in my cabin all summer if she wants to."

"That would look good, wouldn't it?" Rita shook her head. "It just won't do. You're forgetting your reputation, partner."

"Oh hell," Sarboe said in disgust. "I haven't heard you worry about that before."

Rita laughed and patted his arm. "My friend, the only woman I trust is Rita Gentry."

"I'm not after your man and I won't beg," Linda breathed. "All I want is a chance to make my way."

"Sure." Sarboe held up his hands to her. "We'll find something for you to do."

Linda stepped down, holding to his hands as a wave of nausea swept over her. Too much had happened today. Breaking with Mike had been the biggest decision she had ever made. She closed her eyes, swaying as doubts rose to plague her. She had been a fool to come here. She should have known.

Rita was shaking her. "Don't faint. Don't faint, I tell you." She shook Linda again. "Want me to get the doctor?"

"I'm all right." Linda put her hand to her throat. "I'm all right. I just feel sort of wrung out."

"Can you walk?" Sarboe asked.

"Yes. I'm all right I tell you. I never faint." Her eyes touched Rita's. "I'm stronger than I look."

"You'd better be if you're going to stay here," Rita said. "Let's take her to your cabin, Ben. She needs to lie down."

They walked along the street, Sarboe leading Linda's mare, Rita's arm around Linda's small waist. When they reached the cabin, Rita said, "Go get your fishing pole, Ben. She'll rest better if she has the cabin to herself for an hour or two."

Sarboe gave her a questioning look. "You're about as changeable as the weather."

"It's a woman's constitutional right to change her mind, pardner. Go on now while I put on another dress."

Sarboe led Linda's mare toward the barn as Rita stepped into the cabin. She said, "You lie down on the bunk, Linda. Stay there till I get back. You gave me a turn just now."

Linda crossed the cabin to the bunk. "I'm really all right. I guess I got scared. There just wasn't any place for me to go. I know I shouldn't have come here, but Mr. Sarboe told me to come if I couldn't stay in Dallamville."

Rita unbuttoned her dress and slipped out of it. "So Mr. Sarboe said that, did he?" She laughed. "Well, don't let it give you ideas. Ben's just naturally friendly to good-looking women and stray pups. Anyhow, you can quit being scared. You can stay here as long as you want to."

Linda said nothing for a moment, her eyes on Rita's tall, perfectly proportioned body. Then she blurted, "I don't blame him for liking you. You're beautiful."

Rita was stepping into a tan skirt when Linda said that. She straightened, surprised, and almost tripped before she regained her balance. She said, "Now let's get one thing straight now. I don't take to being hoorawed about my looks."

"I mean it."

Rita slipped into a shirtwaist, turning her head to give Linda a searching look. "No woman ever said that to me before, and I'd never say it to another woman if I meant it." She buttoned her shirtwaist, adding, "You'll get along."

"You've been staying here?"

"Just till the hotel is open. Don't get mixed up on things. Ben's been sleeping in the barn. We're partners, business partners. That's all."

"You'll be more than that," Linda said. "Please believe one thing. You don't have to be jealous about me."

"That's one thing I can believe." Rita gave her skirt a final adjustment and patted her hair. "It's like I said. Ben and I are partners. That's all. Now you lie down and rest."

Linda did not get up until Rita had left. Then she rose and, walking to the window, watched them cross the meadow to the river. Rita was looking at Sarboe and laughing. *They belong together*, Linda thought. *They fit whether they know it or not*. She shook her head, frowning, and said aloud, "I wonder if she's really fooling herself."

Turning to the stove, she started a fire, then filled a pan with water and put it on to heat. There were dishes to be washed. It was a good way to start earning her keep. She stood by the stove, waiting, her troubled thoughts turning again to Mike. She wondered if her leaving would force a break between him and Dallam, and knew at once that it would not.

Chapter X

FIRST SETTLER

THE FOLLOWING Monday morning Sarboe ate breakfast in the tent dining room. He had slept later than he intended to and he hurried with his meal. Both Rita and Purvane had eaten. Purvane had gone to the ditch and Rita, Sarboe guessed, would be working in the office.

He wanted to see her. There was something he had to say, although he did not know how he would say it. She had irritated him the evening before after they had returned to the cabin. They had spent two hours on the river, fishing upstream from the meadows. He had hooked four rainbows and she had caught one, and it seemed to him that she had enjoyed every minute of the two hours.

But he had noticed a change in her after they had returned to the cabin and had supper. Nothing definite that he could lay his hands on, just a feeling that came from the way she said things rather than the words she used. He had no understanding of the secret weapons that women use upon one another, but he sensed the sparring that had gone on between Rita and Linda, and Rita, because she was the stronger, had been successful in pushing Linda into the background.

But Sarboe had no opportunity to see Rita alone that morning. As he left the dining tent, the butcher called that he needed three steers.

"Right away," Sarboe said, and turned toward his barn.

He was saddling up when Linda said, "Good morning, Ben."

He stepped out of the stall and touched his hat brim. "Morning, Linda. How do you feel?"

"Fine. I'm sorry about yesterday. I'm really not as puny as I seemed. All of a sudden everything caught up with me, I guess."

He rolled a smoke, knowing he should be on his way but not wanting to go. She was a small, proud girl, standing in the doorway with the morning sun to her back, her head held high. She had been afraid when she had ridden into town yesterday, but this morning he sensed no fear in her.

"I've been thinking about a job for you," he said. "I'm postmaster, you know. Lately I've been crowded a little, so I thought maybe you'd take care of it for me. Wouldn't pay much, but you could stay in the cabin."

"Thank you, Ben," she said, "but Rita wouldn't like it."

He frowned. "That's no reason to turn it down. Rita can't run everything."

"You're kind," she said slowly. "Let me think about it. I'm not sure what I should do."

He fired his cigarette, nodding. "And while you're thinking it over, you've got a place to stay."

Sarboe stepped into the stall and backed his horse into the runway. Linda said, "Wait, Ben. There's something I've got to say."

"I'm listening. Got both ears up."

She laughed, then her face was grave again. "I keep hoping that my running away will change Mike, then I stop to think about it and I know it won't. But what I wanted to tell you was that before I left, I heard some talk between Dallam and Verd Ricket." She told him about it, adding, "I don't know what they meant, but I thought you would."

He shook his head. "No, but we'll find out before long. We've been sliding along too easy. Well, I've got to ride. You stick here. If Mike comes after you, don't go back unless you want to."

"I won't," she said, "and I don't think Mike will come after me."

She turned away quickly and walked to the cabin. Mounting, he rode into the timber. He did not look at her. He knew that she was crying and he understood how it was with her. She had picked her road; she had given Mike her back. It would never be the same between them again.

It was nearly noon when Sarboe brought the steers in. Ordinarily he would have helped with the butchering, but before he could swing out of the saddle, Lou Fain yelled, "Sarboe, Rita wants you."

Sarboe winked at the butcher. "Sure sorry, Jim, but it sounds like I'm needed somewhere else."

"You're sorry like hell," the butcher snorted. "You're needed in too damned many places."

Fain came up, wheezing as he always did after a fast walk. He said, "Rita's got a settler in the office with a chip on his shoulder. Better get over there."

"You're too fat, Lou," Sarboe said. "You'll lose fifty pounds bringing in that bear."

The lawyer wiped a hand across his sweat-beaded forehead. "I like me the way I am," he grunted. "It's the damned altitude."

"Altitude," Sarboe jeered. "You'd better get out of here or Jim will make steaks out of you. You're in prime condition."

"Better'n the steers you fetched in," the butcher agreed.

Sarboe rode away, grinning. He liked Fain. Some of the others, Otis Barrett particularly, had too much dignity to take a little rawhiding, but Fain could.

Sarboe wondered about the settler as he tied in front of the townsite office and went in. There would be no water on the land until fall, perhaps not until spring. A settler now was as unexpected as a robin in January. Dozens of men were drifting in, but they were looking for work, not land.

Rita was standing by her desk, and Sarboe saw at once that she was angry. That surprised him, for she was not one to show her feelings in front of a prospective customer. When she saw Sarboe, she said curtly, "Mr. Packard, this is my partner, Ben Sarboe." She nodded at Sarboe. "Mr. Packard thinks we're crooks."

Packard made a slow turn and held out his hand. "That ain't quite right, Mr. Sarboe. I'm just asking questions."

Sarboe shook Packard's calloused hand. He was a burly man with square-tipped fingers and arms as big as the average man's legs. Brown eyes were pinned on Sarboe appraisingly; a flowing yellow mustache dropped on both sides of a meaty-lipped mouth. Some men like George Dallam could not be read, but this Packard seemed to have no guile in him. It was Sarboe's feeling that he was basically honest, but cautious.

"Miss Gentry has the answers." Sarboe motioned toward a chair. "Sit down, Packard, while you ask the questions."

Packard shook his head. "I'll stand." He shoved his big hands into his pants pockets. "I left my woman and my fifteen-year-old boy in a wagon. It's up the street a piece. We've been dry farming in Eastern Washington till I got burned out. Sold my place and was headed for the Willamette Valley when I heard about this country. We figured we'd take a look at it. If we don't like it, we can go on over the Santiam Pass to the Willamette Valley."

"We ain't stopping you," Sarboe said.

"I know that." Packard gave him a slow grin. "Nobody's stopping me, but you see, I kind of like what I've seen around here. Sandy soil, but if a man don't get a piece of land that's mostly lava rock, he oughta make a living." He waggled a thick finger at Sarboe. "Providing he has water and plenty of it."

"That's what's biting him," Rita said irritably.

Sarboe understood now. The one thing Rita could not stand was the insinuation that she was dishonest. He said quickly, "You'll have water, but if you have any doubts that you will, don't settle here."

"You don't have no right to tell me that," Packard said. "This is government land, not yours. It's up to you to furnish the water."

"You expect us to take the risks and do the work and give you the water free?" Rita demanded.

Packard shook his head. "No, I don't expect anything of the kind, but I've got a right to know whether water will be so damned high that I can't make a living. Then there's the railroad. I hear talk all over the country about it, but I ain't sure Harriman will ever build south of Shaniko."

"We won't be sure until we hear a locomotive's whistle right here in Swift River," Sarboe said, "but we can be mighty sure that when Harriman figures there's enough stuff to be hauled in and out of this country to make him a profit, he'll build."

Rita sat down on her desk and leaned back, both hands behind her head. "Listen, friend. What happens in this country depends on you and ten thousand like you who are willing to gamble. We're gambling, plenty."

"And about the cost of water," Sarboe said. "We don't know what it will be, but it'll be high. You can't build a ditch through a lava country like this for pennies."

Packard stepped back so he could see both Rita and Sarboe. He said a little uncomfortably, "I guess what really gets under my hide is having to do business with a purty woman. My notion of what a woman ought to be doing is keeping house and raising kids."

"My being a woman has nothing to do with how many potatoes you can raise per acre," Rita said testily. "You'll have your water."

Rita slid off the desk and moved around it to her chair. She sat down, a gesture of dismissal which Packard did not take. He was a slow-thinking man, Sarboe judged, but once his mind was made up, it would not be easily changed.

"I want to settle here," Packard said, "but I aim to get some answers before I do. I've got a little money which has come damned hard." He glanced at Rita apologetically. "Excuse me, ma'am. What I mean is I got cleaned in '93. Made me plumb mad, the government messing around with silver like it done because some Eastern capitalists said gold was good and silver wasn't. I was in Colorado at the time . . ."

"We came from Cripple Creek," Sarboe broke in.

"Well, I declare," Packard said, pleased. "Kind of a small country, now ain't it? Of course Cripple Creek wasn't hit, being a gold camp, but the state as a whole was. It wasn't right, no way you look at it. Well, here we are." He held up big, calloused hands. "I've got these, a wife, and a boy. The little bit of money I've got don't make no big difference. It's you folks who have a lot of money who make the difference."

Rita had opened a ledger. Suddenly she pushed it back with a sharp, angry motion. Sarboe expected her to explode, but he saw that she was keeping control of her temper.

"Mr. Packard," Rita said, "I know how you feel. Please believe that. Every man who comes here will feel the same way, but your trouble is that you're looking at this from your standpoint only. That's not right."

"We've got to look out for number one," Packard shouted. "Nobody ever looked out for Bill Packard but Bill Packard."

Rita leaned forward. "Perhaps, but don't forget that we're putting our hearts and souls into this project along with our money. We want a prosperous country. We've got to have it if we're going to prosper."

Packard scratched the back of his neck. He said grudgingly, "Hadn't thought of it just that way. Maybe it's a good idea, having a woman in . . ."

A wagon rolled into town from the east, the driver whipping a lathered team and yelling above the rattle of the wagon, "Doc! Doc! Get out here, Doc."

Sarboe turned through the door just as Doc Zachary lunged out of his office, black bag in hand, and came toward the wagon in a lumbering run. The driver pulled up as others crowded around, and Sarboe saw that the driver was one of Purvane's men.

"Hell busted loose on the ditch," the driver cried. "That's Ben Lane back there, what's left of him."

An unconscious man lay in the bed of the wagon. Sarboe took one look at his face and turned away, sick. He had seen many brutal fights; he had seen men beaten up so badly that he could not recognize them, but he had never seen a human face like Ben Lane's, a mass of cuts and bruises and clotted blood.

Zachary handed his bag to Otis Barrett. "Fetch that, Otis. Here, give me a hand with him, Lou."

Carefully, Zachary and Lou Fain lifted the unconscious man from the wagon and carried him to the doctor's office. Sarboe looked up at the white-faced driver. "Who did it, Carter?"

"Fellow named Verd Ricket. Signed on this morning. Right off he started getting ornery. Told us we wasn't getting paid what we should. Said we oughta have our women and kids in camp instead of here in town where we couldn't see 'em except on Sundays. Purvane fired him, but he wouldn't go. Knocked Purvane cold. Then Lane tied into him, and that's what happened."

This, then, was what Dallam and Verd had planned, and Purvane, not knowing Verd, had fallen into it. Sarboe turned from the wagon and walked to his horse. He had told Linda that things had been sliding along too easily. This was the end of the easy sliding. Dallam had made a smart move. Anything that Verd Ricket did could not be legally held against Dallam.

Sarboe did not know that Rita was there until she gripped his arm. "What is it Ben?"

"Trouble," he said. "Big trouble."

"What are you going to do?"

He looked at her worried face, wondering how much she could read in his. "I've got to get Verd Ricket, or you won't have any crew to dig a ditch."

"I'll go, too."

"No. Trouble was my part of the bargain. You stay here and take care of your end."

Pulling free from her grip he turned and mounted. He rode away, not sure what he could do. Luck had been with him the first time he had tangled with Verd, luck and Cap Ricket. Verd was a man who would use his fists and his boots, not his gun, and this time Cap would not be there.

Chapter XI

THE FIGHT

NOTHING was being done on the ditch. Sarboe knew that before he was in sight of the camp, for there was a great deal of rock work to be done and usually the roar of dynamite could be heard when a man was a long way off. He topped a ridge and looking down upon the camp, saw what he had been sure he would see, idle horses and idle men. Not a scraper or wagon was moving, not a pick or shovel was being lifted.

There were about two hundred men in camp. Part of them were the carefully picked, loyal men Purvane had brought to Swift River the night after Rita had first come, but the majority were transients. Most of these had families that were living in covered wagons or tents in Swift River, for Purvane had laid down one rule from the first; women and children were not allowed to live in or near the construction camp.

There were single men, too, with no roots to hold them. A few quit every day, others drifted in to take their places, intending to work only for a week or perhaps a month before their fiddle feet took them on to another job. It was a situation Sarboe understood, for mining camps were little different.

The single men were the ones who would give him the trouble. He had heard some complaints that Swift River was a Sunday School town where it was hard to get a drink or find a woman. Verd Ricket would take advantage of that discontent and many of the single men would support him just for the hell-raising he promised if for no better reason.

As Sarboe rode down the slope toward the long line of freshly moved earth and broken rock and uprooted junipers that wound worm-like toward the river, he saw that the situation was closer to the exploding point than he had supposed. Verd Ricket stood at the head of a closely packed knot of men. The rest formed a long half-circle from the ditch to the dining tent. Purvane was with them, his face showing the hammering that Verd's fists had given him, but he was still on his feet.

No one paid any attention to Sarboe as he rode up. Verd was beating his right fist into the palm of his left hand as he cursed Purvane in a great, bellowing voice. The majority of the men were standing behind Purvane, but Sarboe saw the difference at once between the two groups.

A few were from the original crew that Purvane had brought with him. Ben Lane had been one of them. Even these men, tied as they were to Rita and Purvane by tight bonds of loyalty, did not want any part of the fight. The memory of the brutal beating Verd had given Lane was too fresh in their minds.

The rest of the men standing back of Purvane were the family men who acted as if they were spectators. Sarboe counted them out at once. The smaller group backing Verd were the toughs, the drifters who didn't think as far as the next pay day and didn't give a damn whether a ditch was dug or not.

Purvane's face had never been more melancholy than it was now. He had been whipped once today, but still he had the look of a man who was bound to try again and knew he would fail. He stood motionless, listening, for Verd was not giving him a chance to say anything.

It was only when Verd stopped his ranting to take a breath that Sarboe was able to break in, "How much is Dallam paying you for this, Verd?"

Verd Ricket had been watching Purvane so closely that he was not aware of Sarboe's presence until that instant. He wheeled to face Sarboe, a pleased look on his knobby, scarred face. He said, "Well, if it ain't the star-toting postmaster. What in hell are you doing here, bucko, looking for the mail?"

"I saw Ben Lane," Sarboe said. "What's going on, Fred?"

Sarboe had never seen a more relieved man than Purvane was. He wiped a sleeve across his sweaty face and sucked in a long breath. Then he shouted, "This fellow is raising hell, that's what's happening. I've never had any labor trouble and I don't know why I'm having it now. The boys don't have a kick. Not any of 'em."

"The hell we don't," a redhead behind Verd shouted. "You're running Swift River, but we've got to go to Prineville to have any fun. That's plenty to kick about."

"There's something else," a man standing next to the ditch called. "I'm married, but it don't do me much good. Purvane says my wife stays in town. I see her Saturday nights and Sundays. That's all, and I say it ain't right."

Purvane gestured wearily. "We've been over this ten times, Fryer. That rule is for the good of your wives and kids. If I let one man have his family here, I've got to let 'em all. It's too dangerous with the blasting we're having every day."

"My wife knows enough to stay away from the ditch," Fryer said belligerently.

"The kids don't," Purvane said. "Besides, Doc Zachary tells me there's more danger of an epidemic if we keep the kids in camp. They're safer in town where the doc can see 'em right off if they get the sniffles."

"Got it all figured, ain't you?" Verd asked. "Well, it don't make no sense to me. I ain't married, but if I was, I'd want my woman where I could sleep with her every night. Looks to me like it's just a damned trick to make all of you boys eat in their mess hall."

"You're a lying son of a . . ." Purvane began.

"This what the trouble is over, Fred?" Sarboe cut in.

Purvane shook his head. "Wages mostly. We're paying as good as a man can get anywhere, but right off Ricket started hollering for three dollars a day. He didn't sign on to work. He just wants to make trouble."

"It's time somebody was making trouble," Verd shouted. "You're making plenty, Sarboe, you and that woman of yours. I say it's time you was splitting with them that do the work." He cuffed back his battered Stetson. "Now tell me something, bucko. How do you figure this is any business of the law?"

"If Ben Lane dies, it'll be murder." Sarboe waved a hand toward the ditch. "Right now I'm talking as part owner of the ditch company, not as a deputy. We're paying all we can afford to pay. Any chuckle-headed fool would know we can't give three dollars a day to a man without a team. If you don't want to work, dust."

"We want to work," a man said, "but we aim to get a square deal."

Ignoring him, Sarboe hipped around in his saddle and motioned to the men in the line behind Purvane. "Get back on the job. If you don't want to, light out for town and draw your time. We'll get men in here who do want to work."

"Hold on, Sarboe," a man called. "Most of us ain't hollering for more money. There wasn't no trouble till Ricket showed up. He says he'll beat hell out of the first man who touches a shovel handle. We seen what happened to Lane."

"It'll happen to you, too, friend," Verd bawled. "We've got to hang together if we're gonna get our rights."

"You ain't fooling nobody," Sarboe said. "I asked you a while ago how much Dallam was paying you to kick up this fuss."

"Dallam?" Verd shook his head. "Never heard of the man. I live here. I was in the country a hell of a long time before you or Purvane or that yaller-headed woman of yours was. I just want a chance to work for a fair wage."

Sarboe drew his gun. "You're lying, Verd." He nodded at Purvane. "It ain't no mystery why he showed up today. He's working for Dallam and Kelly. Dallam figures to stop work on the ditch and bust us. Then he thinks he'll take over what we've done for a song."

"You're the liar," Verd bawled. "I don't know Dallam or Kelly." He motioned to the men behind him. "Boys, this here is a government proposition. The company aims to get its ditch dug for nothing and then rob the settlers when it sells 'em the water. We'll fight or crawl. Which is it going to be?"

"We'll fight," the redhead yelled. "We ain't got nothing to lose."

"Nothing but your life." Sarboe pulled back the hammer of his gun. "I aim to see that them who want to work can work. I'll kill the first man who tries to stop them."

The forward movement behind Verd stopped. One look at Sarboe's face was enough. Even Verd stood motionless, big hands shoved into his pockets, head tipped forward a little. He said, "Get down off that horse, bucko. We'll settle this, you and me."

Sarboe shook his head. "I didn't come here to fight. I want to keep the work going. That's all."

Verd's head tipped a little lower, his knobby face as bright with anticipation as a saloon bum's who has just been handed a silver dollar for whiskey.

"You're setting real good, ain't you, Sarboe?" Verd asked. "Here's honest men who ain't allowed to be with their wives, but you stay in town, toting your star and strutting like a rooster while your woman sleeps in your cabin. Purty, ain't it? Real purty. Why, if I was one of these married men . . ."

"All right, Verd," Sarboe said, and stepped down.

Sarboe did not recognize his own voice. If Verd Ricket had been carrying a gun, he would have died then, but Verd knew his strength and his weakness. He had nursed his hatred from the moment Sarboe had knocked him down, so he had said the one thing that he knew would bring Sarboe out of his saddle.

"Don't like it, do you, Sarboe?" Verd pressed. "You don't like to hear it. I wouldn't, either, if I had a good thing like you've got."

Sarboe handed his gun to Purvane. "There's five shells in that iron, Fred. Shoot the first five men who try to back Ricket."

"Kill the lying son," Purvane choked. "Kill that lying filthy-mouthed son."

Verd laughed, his great head thrown back, black eyes bright with wickedness. "So you're going to kill me, bucko. I want to see that. I sure as hell want to see you do that."

Sarboe shucked out of his coat and tossed it and his gun belt to one side, movements slow and deliberate. He took off his hat and laid it on his coat, then he walked toward Verd. At this moment there was no power in him to think, to plan, to consider his chances. For the first time in his life he wanted to kill a man with his bare hands, to beat him into the dirt and jump on him and scar his face with his boots, to tear Verd's jugular vein out of his throat with his fingers.

Verd did not move. He had been in two fights this morning, but there was not a mark on his face. He still stood with his thick legs spread, his hands in front of him now, and when Sarboe was close, he said in a low tone, "You won't get me like you done before, bucko."

Sarboe said nothing. When he was a step away he let go with a right that caught Verd on the nose and brought a burst of blood splashing across his face. He let out an involuntary squall of pain; he grabbed Sarboe around the middle and squeezed. From that moment Sarboe had no knowledge of the cheers that rose from the circle around them, no knowledge of Purvane's orders to stand back and let them alone. Ben Sarboe was fighting for several things, and among them was his life.

Verd intended to hang on and squeeze the breath out of Sarboe, but he was never able to put his real strength into the squeeze. Sarboe had both hands free, and they worked on Verd's face with the speed and precision of a hammering piston, short wicked blows that rocked Verd's head and hurt him. Then he slammed his right knee up into Verd's crotch and Verd let go, groaning and sick with agony.

Sarboe never let up. A right to Verd's mouth knocked a tooth loose, a left to his hard-muscled belly brought wind out of his great lungs. Another man would have been finished then, but Verd Ricket had a bull's strength. He fell forward, hands on Sarboe again, and brought him down into the dust. They went over, Sarboe on top, fists still hammering, on over again and Verd batted Sarboe in the face with his head.

A thousand pinwheels exploded before Sarboe's eyes. Verd had him by the throat, choking him. Sarboe got his thumbs into the man's eyes and pressed, and again sheer pain made Verd relinquish his grip. Sarboe arched his body and rolled the man off.

It was a fight they still talk about on the Deschutes, a fight without rules and without decency, a fight between two animals of the wilderness. Sarboe rose and jumped on Verd before he got up, boots driving into his belly. Verd grabbed him by a leg and upended him, a hard fall that threw him among the rocks at the edge of the ditch. It jarred and hurt, and before he could regain his feet, Verd kicked him in the ribs.

Afterwards Sarboe had no clear recollection of the rest of the fight. His shirt was torn off, his face was bleeding from a dozen cuts, his bruised and hammered body hurt from skull to toes. Still, he regained his feet and got out of the rocks and back to level footing. Verd picked up a piece of lava rock and threw it. Sarboe ducked and rammed into Verd's middle, head down like a charging bull.

Verd gave ground. Sarboe pursued him, each breath a labored pant. Verd's guard was down; he swung a ponderous blow that Sarboe ducked, and Sarboe caught him squarely on the point of his chin. Verd fell, slowly at first like a great pine beginning to topple, then every control seemed to go at once and he sprawled full length, bloody face in the churned-up dirt.

Sarboe's strength was almost gone; he fell and struggled back up to his hands and knees and crawled toward Verd.

Purvane yelled, "He's done, Ben. He's done fighting."

Still Sarboe kept crawling. He reached Verd's motionless body and struck at him. Purvane motioned to the men behind him. "Pull him off before he does kill the ornery son."

They lifted Sarboe to his feet. He struck at them. A man grabbed his arm, saying, "Stop it, Sarboe. You licked hell out of him. Stop it."

He stared at them glassy-eyed, laboring for each breath that seemed to stick in his throat, then his knees gave and he sagged in their hands.

"Get a wagon, Dennis," Purvane called. "He needs the doc. Damn that Ricket to hell." He swung to the men who had backed Verd, "Git. You're fired. Git, or I'll dust you off with lead. Take Ricket with you. Go work for Dallam if he wants your kind."

They went as if dazed by what had happened. The wagon rolled up and Purvane helped lift Sarboe into the bed. "Take it easy, Dennis. He's hurt pretty bad." Purvane wiped his face, the gun dangling in his hand at his side. Then he added, "Rita didn't lie about you, boy. You'll do."

Purvane stepped back, waving the wagon on. He watched it go, his lean face gray and pinched with worry. This was not the end. It was only the beginning.

Chapter XII

INTERLUDE

FOR A LONG TIME Ben Sarboe lay on his bunk, living in a dark and shadowy world and knowing little that went on around him. Doc Zachary came in twice a day to look at him. Then he would shake his head and go away. Abe Tottle had sent a cot from the store for Linda to sleep on. Rita had moved to the hotel, but she took her turn beside the bunk during the night while Linda slept. There were no hard words between them. Instead there was a cool truce that only once was seriously threatened.

It was one evening after Zachary had said, "We're lucky. Ben will be all right if you can keep him quiet. Maybe he'll never know it, but he owes his life to his two nurses."

Zachary had left then, and Linda had walked away from the bunk, crying. Rita watched her, a little scornfully as a strong person looks upon a weaker one. She said, "You love him, don't you."

Linda whirled. "Of course I do."

"Well, maybe you'll get him. The funny part of it is you'll make him a good wife. You won't fight with him. You'll give him anything he wants at any time he wants it, and I wouldn't be surprised if you made him happy."

Linda walked back toward the bunk, her face very pale. There were no tears on her cheeks now. She stopped a step away from the taller woman and looked defiantly at her. "If I ever get to be his wife, I'll make him a good one, but I won't have the chance. I lack something he needs. You have it, but you don't have sense enough to know it. Or maybe you're such a fool that your pride won't let you admit it."

"He had his chance," Rita said roughly. "If he wanted me, he'd have taken it. And I'm not going to give in to him all the time. I suppose that before we're done, we'll have a row that'll break us up and I'll have to buy him out. Then I'll be broke and it'll make me a bigger fool than even you think I am."

"I hope it works out that way," Linda said slowly, "but I know it won't."

"Why?"

"Because you love him. You'll go on giving in to him."

"The hell I will," Rita said hotly. "I know what I want."

"No you don't. You don't know what you really want. You've lived with men so long you've learned to swear like them and sometimes you think like them, but you're still a woman and you've got a woman's heart. In the end you'll listen to it."

At that moment Rita hated Linda Kelly with every nerve and fiber that was in her. Linda was small and cuddly and at times a little helpless. Ben had been drawn to her from the first day he had seen her or he wouldn't have ridden back to Dallamville with her to see Mike Kelly.

Rita turned away, saying, "Get some sleep, Linda."

She was not as strong as she had been a moment before. Old memories crowded into her mind, the hunger for Ben that she had tried so desperately to kill. She had tried to substitute something else, but it hadn't worked and it never would.

Rita sat down beside the bunk, her back turned to Linda who had started to undress, and hate grew in her until it was a poison in her veins. She thought of the doctor's words, "He owes his life to his two nurses." It was something she would share with Linda Kelly all her years, and she didn't want to share anything with Linda.

She sat motionless, her hands folded on her lap as she looked at Ben's face, very thin and pale now, at the bandage around his head. It was the head injury that had been dangerous. He had fallen in the rocks during the fight, Purvane had said, and he had suffered a concussion. How he had been able to keep on fighting was a mystery to everyone.

The bruises on his face had healed; his broken ribs would inconvenience him for a time, but it was the head injury which was still touchy. *He had to be kept quiet.* Zachary had said it a dozen times. That was why someone was always beside the bunk, for at times he was fretful and he needed assurance that everything was all right. His bodily needs must be attended to. When he asked for a drink, he had to have it at once. Then he would usually drop back to sleep.

It had been her fault that he had taken this beating. The knowledge sent a chill raveling down her spine. She had done a fair job of living in the manner she wanted to live, of flouting conventions and making her way in a man's world. Now the results had caught up with her.

Purvane had told her how it had been. Ben had pulled his gun and he would have handled the situation without real trouble if Verd Ricket had not said, "You stay in town while your woman sleeps in your cabin." Those words had brought him down out of his saddle to fight Ricket with his hands.

Her laced fingers tightened until her knuckles were white. She hated the rules of propriety that bound her, rules she had sworn she would ignore. She had done exactly that. After her father had died she had started out with Fred Purvane. In time she had gathered the others: John Meacham, Otis Barrett, Lou Fain, Abe Tottle. Good men for their jobs, men who saw things the way she did. It had always been a matter of pride with her that she was able to bend them to her will. It had always paid them financially to allow themselves to be bent, and there were times when she wondered how it would be if her luck ran sour.

She had long ago proved to her own satisfaction what she wanted to prove, that a woman could do anything a man could. Big things, worthwhile things like building a town and making the desert a fit home for men and their families. It had been a dream with her that had grown through the years. Now the dream was being transformed into solid houses and streets and business buildings; into a ditch that would carry water to the thirsty soil. But there was one strange thing about it that she could not understand. The satisfaction that the dream had promised was not in her now.

Without turning her head to look she knew that Linda was in bed and asleep. She envied Linda the ability to go to sleep the instant she had a chance. It enabled her to look after Ben three times as many hours as Rita could. That was wrong, too. Before dawn she would wake Linda and go to her hotel room. She would lie down on a far better bed than this bunk where she had slept so soundly, but sleep would prove evasive.

It had been that way from the afternoon when they had brought Ben's battered body and laid him on his bunk. She would lie on her back, staring into the darkness, and presently gray dawn light would creep in through the east window. She would drop off finally and then Abe Tottle would climb the stairs and pound on her door. It would be time to start another day.

Now, in the thin light from the low-turned lamp on the table, she looked at Ben's pale wedge of a face. She could hardly see the white crescent-shaped scar on his jaw. Before the fight the scar had stood out, making a sharp contrast with the dark tan of his face. She wondered if he would be different when he was well. He had gone far down into that strange intermediate land between life and death. It was likely that he would be changed. That was only human. He might be . . . she mentally searched for the right word. Pliable! That was it.

She hated herself then; she hated her own will and pride, her instinctive desire to dominate. She didn't want Ben Sarboe to change. He had changed from their days together in Cripple Creek until now he was not like any other man she had ever met. She had not realized that when she had talked to him here in this cabin that first night, when they had made their bargain and she had kissed him and told him to forget she was a woman. She had not supposed he would take her at her word the way he had. She understood now how impossible were the things she had wanted, impossible because Ben Sarboe was the man he was and she was the woman she was.

It had been natural enough for Verd Ricket to say what he had. Probably other people thought the same thing. Well, she was out of the cabin now, but Linda was here. Linda, who loved him and had given so much to him. Linda, who had changed his bedding and his clothes and bathed him. Linda, who had shared an intimacy with him that Rita had not shared because she lacked the time.

What would happen after he was well? Linda had no money. Or very little. But she couldn't stay here. She must be made to see that. It would lead to more trouble. With her brother Mike if not anyone else. He had been in Swift River twice since the fight, but both times Linda had told him flatly that she would never go back to him until he broke with Dallam and Kelly swore that was the last thing he would ever do and Linda had no right to ask it.

There was one way out. Rita would have to see that Linda had a job. The hotel was the answer. There were other women who needed work, women whose husbands were not making enough to buy warm clothes and the right food and pay Doc Zachary when he was called to doctor the children through the measles and typhoid and croup.

Rita had balanced this in her mind many times and she always came to the one answer that instinctively struck her as being wrong. Linda must have the job in the hotel.

She rose stiffly from the chair. She was tired, more tired than she had ever been before in her life, more tired even than she had been yesterday and that seemed impossible. Moving to the door, she opened it and stared across the meadow to the river, then lifted her eyes to the sky and the million stars that it held. A sense of guilt crept into her. She had tried to play God and she wasn't big enough. Not nearly big enough.

When she turned back in to the house, she glanced at the clock and saw that it was time to wake Linda. She had been with her thoughts at Ben's bedside longer than she had realized. She moved across the room to the cot and shook Linda's shoulder.

Linda woke at once and sat upright. "Ben all right?"

"Of course. He hasn't moved for hours."

Rita turned and walked past the table to the door. She paused there a moment, her eyes on Linda, wondering if she should say that she was going to tell Abe Tottle to give Linda a job in the hotel and decided not. She'd talk to Tottle first. She went out quickly, closing the door behind her.

As she walked back to the hotel, she could hear the mutter of the river which was running higher than usual because of the melting snow in the mountains. As she moved along the silent street between the false fronts, dark, unfriendly walls pressing against her in the blackness, she wondered if the river ever got tired, working on its job for an eternity. It must. She was tired, and she had been working on hers only a few weeks.

She turned in to the hotel and climbed the stairs, each step squeaking underfoot, shrill and loud in the stillness. She walked down the hall to her room, smiling a little as she passed Curly Hewitt's door. He was the new water man who had come to town only the week before with his team and wagon and barrels. Every morning since he had taken this room she had heard him as she passed his door, snoring as he was now in thunderous rapture, and she had envied him his talent for sleeping just as she envied Linda's.

She went into her room and locked the door. Undressing quickly, she slipped into her nightgown and got into bed, pulling the covers up under her chin. She shivered for a few minutes. The last two nights had been colder than usual, sharp with frost even this late in spring. Then she was warm and she closed her eyes and tried to lull her tired body to sleep, but she could not, for her thoughts started plowing through her mind again.

Chapter XIII

SHAD COREY

STRENGTH was slow to return to Ben Sarboe and his inactivity galled him. It was a paradoxical thing which he did not try to understand. Two months ago he had been satisfied to fish and hunt, to rack the mail and pass it out to the few who came by for it and to talk a few minutes with them, to josh Barney Johns as the stage stopped to pick up the mail and drop off an occasional passenger. He had walked out of life and shut the door behind him. Then Rita Gentry had slammed the door wide open and he had walked back through it.

The thing Sarboe did not understand was his own feelings on the matter. He had resented Mike Kelly's project because he liked this country the way he had found it; he had been reluctant in agreeing to Rita's offer for the same reason.

Now he had time to think about it with Doc Zachary ordering him to be quiet and Linda hovering around like a clucking mother hen. The more he thought about it, the more he was puzzled. His attitude had reversed itself, but not by conscious direction. The job that Rita and Purvane had set for themselves was a good job that needed doing, and he was anxious to get back to his part in it.

Every evening Rita came to sit with him while Linda took a walk. No one stayed through the night with him now. Linda had taken a room in the hotel, but she still came to the cabin early in the morning and remained through the day. It was an insult to Sarboe's pride that his weakness had forced him to submit to this care, a sorry thing for a man who had never been sick a day in his life.

"Linda even tucks me in at night," Sarboe told Doc Zachary one evening when they were alone. "I'm beholden to her and all that, but damn it, I'm all right now. Pull her off my neck."

Zachary snorted. "All right, are you? Want her off your neck, do you? You'd better go fishing and see how quick you'll fall on your nose."

"I aim to go fishing. I feel fine . . ."

"Look, my big-talking friend." Zachary waggled a finger under Sarboe's nose. "You'll stay right here in this cabin till I tell you to start walking. In case you haven't heard, you're lucky to be alive."

Sarboe knew that. His memory of most of the fight was clear, he could recall the things that had happened before the fight, but the weeks in bed had left blurred images upon his memory which refused to come clear. It had been only the last few days that he had been able to carry on an intelligent conversation, or even to think with his usual clarity.

"All right," Sarboe said, "but it sure gravels me to be waited on hand and foot. I've been walking around the room since Sunday. When can I go fishing?"

"Next week if you take it easy between now and then. Linda says your appetite's like a bird's, but nature will take care of that as soon as you get outside. You've lost a lot of weight, Ben." Zachary leaned back in his chair and began filling his pipe, frowning as if undecided whether to say the thing that was in his mind or not. He struck a match and fired his pipe. Then he said, "Ben, do you know why you're alive?"

"Too tough to die, maybe."

"Don't be a fool. No man's that tough." Zachary took the pipe out of his mouth. "You're alive because two women gave you the best nursing I ever had the good fortune to watch. I think you're a fool for luck. Otherwise there wouldn't be two women in the country like this to do a job of nursing."

Sarboe groaned. "It's a hell of a note, Doc. I'm beholden to two women and I can't pay either one of 'em back."

"You ignorant, chuckle-headed, rabbit-brained fool," Zachary cried. "They don't want to be paid back. There are some things on this earth a man can't pay back and this is one."

Sarboe scratched his head. "Am I that bad off between the ears, Doc?"

Zachary grinned. "Almost. I tell you, Ben, I never saw a woman I admire as much as I do Rita. I'm not counting Linda short, either. As soon as she can leave you, I'm giving her a job in my office. If there's any nursing to be done, she'll do it. She's got a touch that few women have, but Rita is, well, sort of magnificent. She's going to do this job and all hell won't stop her. She needs you. That's why you've got to be careful. You'll be as good as ever if you don't start pushing yourself too soon."

"Sure, I'll take all summer."

Zachary hadn't said so, but it struck Sarboe that he thought Rita had helped nurse him because she wanted him back on his feet again. He was a cog in her machine like Fred Purvane and the rest, someone for her to use. Well, it was probably true and he was as big an idiot as

Zachary said for thinking there might be any other reason.

The doctor rose, staring down at the pipe that had gone cold in his hand. "I could fall in love with Rita mighty easy, Ben," he said slowly. "That's probably no big news to you. She does that to a man without trying, but I've got about as much chance with her as Purvane has. In one way I'm sorry for her. She got this notion of showing everybody what a woman can do and she's bound to go ahead with it, but she'd be a damned sight happier if she could fall in love with a man enough to want to live with him and bear his children."

"I guess so," Sarboe said dully, "but I don't reckon she ever will."

Zachary fired his pipe again. "Well, got to go. Going to have a baby in the Tilden tent before midnight. Take it easy and you'll be in shape to help me catch the trout for the barbecue. Meacham's doing his part of the job. We'll have a thousand people here for the Fourth."

"That's good," Sarboe said. "I'll behave."

It was not as hard for him to remain idle as he had thought, for he had more visitors than he had expected and more than Linda wanted. She practically held the clock on them and invited them to leave after a few minutes. When Sarboe protested, she said, "I don't want any trouble with you. Rita and I have brought you this far. We don't want you to backslide."

There was no argument he could give to that. He said, "Doc says I owe my life to you. I don't know how I can pay you back . . ."

"Ben, don't say that." She came to where he was sitting at the table and looked down at him. "You've done more for me than I can ever tell you. I'll always be in your debt."

He scratched his head, puzzled. "Why, that's crazy, I haven't . . ."

"No, it isn't crazy. You gave me a place to live when I didn't have any other place to go. I can make my way now, but I get an all-gone feeling when I think what would have happened to me that first day I came here if you hadn't taken me in.''

He let it drop then. Apparently she had thrived on the hard work of taking care of him. She seemed happier than he had ever seen her. There must, he thought, be something that had taken her mind off Mike. Later that day when Rita came to take Linda's place, Sarboe thought he understood. A man waited outside for Linda and they walked across the meadow toward the river.

"Who is he?" Sarboe asked.

Rita smiled. "Jealous?"

Sarboe's hands fisted. Rita had a way of irritating him at times. Now he felt as if she'd scraped every nerve in his body with a currycomb. He said, "No. I just asked who he is.''

"Calls himself Shad Corey. I don't know anything else about him." Rita bit her lower lip, worry flowing across her face. "I don't like him, Ben. He scares me and I'm not easily scared.''

"What's the matter with him?''

"For one thing he packs a gun. This isn't Cripple Creek. He doesn't need a gun in Swift River. Maybe I'm getting jumpy, but I shiver every time I look at his eyes. They're sort of like two pieces of frost.''

"You figure he's a Dallam man?''

She looked away. "I don't know. Dallam hasn't made a move since the fight, but I learned a long time ago to expect a storm after a quiet spell. It's been quiet too long.''

"This Corey. He's been seeing Linda?''

She nodded. "Quite a bit. Goes walking with her. He rode in a couple of weeks ago on a black gelding.'' She made a gesture as if puzzled by the man. "He doesn't ask for work. Just hangs around town. Gambles some. Drinks a little, but most of the time he's watching as if he expected someone to come along.''

"His black a good horse?''

"I wish I owned him. He's the best horse I've seen since I got here." She smiled ruefully and shook her head. "You can tell me I'm spooked. Maybe I am, but that horse is the kind of animal a man would have who thinks he's got a long, hard ride ahead of him."

Sarboe rose and walked to the door. He stood there, looking across the meadow. Linda and Corey had disappeared. He didn't like it. Not at all. She would have no part of spying or dealing with a Dallam man. She was lonely and Corey was paying attention to her. That wasn't good, either. She deserved the best, and he didn't doubt Rita's estimate of the man.

Rita came to stand beside him. He turned, his shoulders against the jamb. He said, "I haven't thanked you for what you and Linda did for me, but . . ."

"Stop it, Ben." She reached out and took his hand. "You stop it right now. Fred told me about your fight with Ricket. As long as we're alive, I'll be in your debt."

"Oh hell." That was all he could say. She had said very nearly what Linda had, and how could a man talk against that kind of female logic?

It was the next morning that Cap Ricket came. He reined up outside and asked for his mail. Linda sorted through a handful of envelopes and shook her head, "Nothing for you this time, Mr. Ricket."

"Thank you. How's Sarboe?"

"He's still weak, but the doctor says he can go fishing next week."

"Can I talk to him?"

"Why yes, if you don't take long."

Sarboe had been lying down. He rose now and walked to the door, calling, "Howdy, Cap."

Ricket gave him a long, studying stare before he said, "You're thin, Sarboe, but your face ain't marked up like Verd's. I'm glad of that."

Sarboe was surprised. He asked, "Verd go back home?"

"Yeah, for a while," Ricket said with great bitterness, "but not because he loved me or Holt. Just like a rat crawling back into his hole. I'm apologizing for what he done. That'll sound funny to you, coming from me, but I ain't proud of Verd. I just wanted you to know that."

"We had quite a tussle."

Ricket nodded. "I could see that looking at his face. Well, he deserved what he got. When a man fights for himself, I say that's good, but when he fights for another man's pay, that's a hell of a thing."

Without another word, Ricket reined his horse around and rode away. Sarboe, glancing up the street, saw that the stranger, Shad Corey, was watching.

It was Saturday morning before Doc Zachary allowed Sarboe to walk up Main Street. He took a slow pace like a tired old man, pausing to shake hands with Lou Fain and John Meacham and the rest. It amused him, for they acted as if he had been gone from the country and had just returned.

They talked about the things that had happened while he had been laid up, the organization of the town, his appointment as marshal, River Street with its saloons and dance halls. He knew these things, but they were easy subjects of conversation. Actually none of them wanted to talk about the thing that weighed heavily against their minds. Sarboe wasn't being fooled. They expected Dallam to try something big and Sarboe was not in shape to fight.

He stepped into the townsite office and sat down wearily behind the desk that he had never used. Rita had dropped her pencil and leaned back, smiling at him. She asked, "How's the old man of the mountains?"

"Fine. I can lick my weight in wildcats. I'm a ring-tailed wowser. I . . ."

A wagon creaked by in the street, the driver calling, "Water for sale. Water, twenty-five cents a barrel, minnows and pollywogs free."

Sarboe swiveled around in his chair and looked out through the open door. "Who's that?"

"Curly Hewitt. He's our water man." She laughed. "He had a room down the hall from mine, and when I was sitting up with you, I'd get back to my room pretty late. I could hear him snore every time I went by."

Sarboe swung back. "What was I talking about?"

"You were lying about how good you felt."

"Oh yeah. Well, I'll quit lying. I feel like a scarecrow that's just been put through the wringer and I know damned well I look like one."

"You do for a fact," she said.

He rolled a cigarette, thinking that Rita looked tired. She was thinner than when she had come to the Deschutes, and the sparkling vitality that had always been in her was gone. Even her shoulders sagged, something he had not noticed before.

"You're working too hard."

She nodded. "I know, but I'm about to take a vacation. I've got a bookkeeper coming in the first of July. Fred says I think nobody can do the job but me and I guess he's right."

"The first of July is still three weeks . . ."

"I'll make out till then," she said impatiently. "We won't be having many settlers before the Fourth. Oh, you remember that man Packard who was in here the day you had the fight?"

Sarboe nodded. "He ain't a man you could forget."

"No, there's nothing halfway about Bill Packard. He's for you or against you. Now he's for us. He said a man who'd fight like you did must believe in what he was doing, so he took eighty acres three miles out of town."

He gave her a searching look, sensing the question that was in her mind. He said, "I believe in what we're doing, if that's what you're wondering. I just hadn't got around to telling you." Swinging his chair, he looked beyond the row of buildings across the street at the pine-green foothills and the snow peaks beyond. "I was wrong on one thing, Rita. I thought people would change everything, but now I know they won't. Those mountains are just too damned big. There'll always be a piece of wilderness out there."

When he turned to look at her, he saw that she was pleased. She said, "I'm glad, Ben."

He rose. "Well, guess I'll go take a look at River Street."

"Not much to look at," she said bitterly. "It's one thing we've done I don't like, but I guess it couldn't be helped, men being what they are."

"That's right," he said, and left the office.

River Street was exactly what Sarboe had expected. Several buildings were going up, but at the moment a number of saloons were housed in tents. By fall the tents would be gone, but the buildings would remain, shells thrown together as quickly and cheaply as possible.

There was a solidness about Main Street that Sarboe liked, but he was depressed by what he saw here. River Street might have been in another world, exactly like a dozen boom towns he had seen, transient and tawdry, its businessmen profiting by the lusty appetites of men seeking relief from the weariness of work.

Shad Corey stood in front of one of the tent saloons, a cigarette pasted to his lower lip, the smoke shadowing his face. It was the first time Sarboe had been close to him. Now, in one appraising glance, he saw that Rita had been right about him.

Corey was a slender man with a hard, tight-lipped mouth and bullet scar on his right cheek. His eyes were pale blue, frosty and forbidding, as Rita had said. He carried his bone-handled .44 in a tied-down holster low on his right thigh. Everything about him added up to gunman. Sarboe had seen many like him in border towns and Colorado mining camps, but he was the first to make an appearance here on the Deschutes and he seemed entirely out of place.

Sarboe would have moved on without speaking if Corey had not said, "Reckon you're the tough marshal I've been hearing about."

"Not so tough," Sarboe said, and grinned. "Not to-day."

Corey grinned, too, a short curl at the corners of his eyes. "I've heard of you, Sarboe, but you don't look much like I figured. Hell, you could pass for the last piece of wash that just went through the wringer."

"That's the way I feel," Sarboe admitted.

"Took on a little too much." Corey scratched his nose, frowning. "I don't savvy. A man who can handle a gun like they say you can should never use his fists."

"So I've heard," Sarboe said, and would have gone on then if Corey had not held him with a quick gesture.

"I've been wondering about something, Sarboe. Who was the tall gent I saw in front of your cabin the other day? Had a black beard. Big fellow."

"Cap Ricket."

"Ricket." Corey repeated the word as if it meant nothing to him. "Live around here?"

"Got a cattle ranch east of town."

"Live alone?"

"He's got two boys, Verd and Holt. Verd was the one I tangled with."

"So that's who it was. Well, reckon you don't love the Rickets none."

Sarboe shrugged. "I've got nothing against Cap or Holt." He searched Corey's dark barren face, wondering. "Now you can tell me something I've been wondering about. You acquainted with George Dallam?"

Corey shook his head. "Heard of him. That's all." He laughed, a brittle sound like that of dry twigs snapping. "You don't think I belong to him, do you?"

"It was in my mind," Sarboe admitted.

"Then you can forget it."

"I'll take your word for it," Sarboe said, and this time when he moved on, Corey let him go.

Linda was baking a cake when Sarboe returned to the cabin. Flour was on her hands and arms, and there was even a smear on her nose. She laughed when Sarboe came in, embarrassed.

"I thought I'd be done before you got back, Ben," she said.

He dropped into a chair at the table. "I saw the town." He cleared his throat, hating the question he had to ask. He said, "I talked to this fellow Corey. Know him?"

She wheeled from the stove, head back, chin tilted defiantly. "Yes, I know him. I've talked to him and I've gone walking with him, and I like him."

"He's no good for you, Linda. He's no good for anybody."

"You see him for five minutes on the street and you know all that." She laughed nervously. "Seems to me you're jumping at conclusions, Ben."

He shook his head. "I know. In this country a man don't pack a gun like Corey does if he's any good. The smell of the wild bunch is all over him."

She was angry. He saw it in her eyes, in the splash of red that touched her cheek. She whipped her small body around to face the stove.

"You tend to your business and I'll tend to mine. You'll be all right now. Monday I'm starting to work for Doc."

He rose and came to the stove. He put his hands on her shoulders and turned her to face him. "I told you the other day I could never pay back all I owe you, but this is one thing I can do. Don't see Corey any more."

"Don't give me orders, Mr. Sarboe." Her chin was still pointed defiantly at him. "Let's say I cancelled out what I owe you by taking care of you. You've got Rita and I've got Shad."

"I don't have Rita," he said angrily, "but that ain't the point. I don't know why Corey's hanging around, but whatever his reason is, it ain't good. Loving him won't bring you nothing but misery."

His hands were still on her shoulders. She was looking up at him, then she lowered her head and the defiance fled from her. Her arms came around him and she buried her face against his shirt. "Ben, Ben, don't you know? I don't love him. I . . . I don't love him at all, but he's been kind and I've been lonesome."

She began to cry, her arms tightening around him with passionate pressure. He stood that way, motionless, wondering how he had managed to get himself into this position, and he did not know that Rita had come in until she said, "Now what do know about that?"

Linda jumped and stepped away from Sarboe. She whirled back to the stove, saying, "I was just baking a cake. It'll be done in a minute. Sit down, Rita."

"Baking a cake," Rita breathed. "I never saw it done that way before, but it might work. Looks like you had plenty of sweetening."

Sarboe walked toward her. "Shut up now and listen. Has this town of ours got an ordinance forbidding packing guns inside the city limits?"

"No, but we can pass one mighty quick. How soon do you want it?"

"Tonight."

"It will be done."

Sarboe moved past her toward the door. Linda cried, "Where are you going?"

"To see Corey."

"Wait, Ben. The cake's almost . . ."

"Save a piece for me."

"Don't go. You're not strong yet."

"I've been babying myself long enough."

"Let him go," Rita said. "When a man gets interested in putting his arms around a woman, there's not much wrong with him."

Sarboe left, irritated. He found Corey still standing in front of the saloon. He said, "I'm giving you two orders, Corey."

The man's pale brows lifted. "I'm a hard man to give orders to, Marshal."

"You'll take these. Let Linda alone and leave your gun in your room."

Sarboe understood how touchy pride was in a man like Shad Corey. He waited, expecting an explosion, but there was none. Corey said easily, "All right, Marshal, I'll take those orders." He paused, the small smile jerking at the corner of his mouth. "For a while."

Chapter XIV

MURDER

BY THE END OF June Sarboe felt like himself again except for occasional headaches which Zachary said he might have to put up with for a long time. Purvane's ditch was progressing. Dust hung over it like a gray shifting fog. Cuts were dynamited through lava ridges and dry washes were flumed, but Purvane's melancholy expression did not change.

"Before we're done," Purvane said one night in the townsite office, "we'll have to cement every cut we've made. Or flume the main ditch all the way. Don't look like that sand will hold water, and every time we bust through a piece of lava, we get enough cracks to let the whole damned river get away."

Without looking at Sarboe, Rita said, "We'll flume it, Fred. Quit worrying."

Purvane scratched his long jaw, eyes on the ceiling. "How much money have you got, Ben?"

"Oh, two or three hundred dollars."

Purvane grinned. "That'll just about match my pile. Rita, have you got any notion how much it'll cost to put that flume in?"

"No, but I've got enough. I said stop worrying."

Purvane shook his head. "I couldn't do that. All right. We put the flume in. Then what happens to you?"

"You think I'll be broke?"

"That's exactly what I think."

She waved a forefinger under his nose. "Then I'll be broke. It's my money, Mr. Purvane."

He threw up his hands. "All right. Go broke. Then we can all go to work for Dallam."

"I'd rather do that than borrow from Otis Barrett or Abe Tottle."

"You'd better go see Doc Zachary."

"Why?"

"You need glasses. That's why. You're getting so short-sighted you can't see past the end of your pretty nose."

"Oh, shut up, Fred." She turned to Sarboe. "Ben, what's happened to Dallam?"

"I don't know. Dallam and Kelly are both in the country. I've heard that. How's their ditch coming, Fred?"

Purvane snorted. "They've caught up with us, but they ain't making a ditch. They're just scratching out a little furrow. Why hell, if it does hold water, it won't carry enough to irrigate a thousand acres."

"That's what Packard was saying," Rita said. "I'll have Meacham start asking questions in the *Clarion*." She tapped her desk thoughtfully. "Where's Verd Ricket, Ben?"

"Dunno."

"I'm worried. Everything's just been too dandy since your fight. You think Dallam wants us to finish the ditch?"

"Might be," Sarboe said. "Don't forget he made me a proposition."

"Give us enough rope and we'll hang ourselves by going broke. You think that's what he's counting on?"

Sarboe nodded. "That's my guess. Then he could step in and buy the ditch for his own figure."

"He won't get it." Rita's lips tightened. "We're selling a few lots, and before another month's out, we'll be settling farmers on our segregation. I'm counting on this Fourth of July celebration to bring us a lot of business."

"That reminds me," Sarboe said. "Lou Fain won't go bear hunting."

Rita smiled. "Didn't expect him to, did you?"

"No, but I had some fun joshing him about it. Can you find a couple of men who will, Fred?"

Purvane nodded. "I've got a couple of boys who are always bragging that they're good hunters. I'll send 'em out in the morning and tell 'em not to come back till they get a bear."

"Doc and me are going fishing in the morning. We'll need a wagon and some ice. How about that, Fred?"

"I'll send some boys to the ice cave in the morning. You'll have it the night of the second. Where do you want it?"

"Below the falls."

"It'll be there."

After Purvane had gone Sarboe waited until Rita had locked the office. He said, "You're worrying about Dallam, but this Shad Corey is the one who's got me scared."

She turned toward the hotel, Sarboe walking beside her. She was silent for a moment, then she said, her voice frosty, "He's keeping away from Linda like you told him. That ought to make you happy."

"Well, it don't. He didn't come here to see Linda, and he ain't hanging around town on her account, but he's here for something." They were silent again for a time, then he said, "You don't need to get hot just because you saw Linda with her arms around me that time."

"I'm not, partner. I'm not hot at all. I'm just wondering why you don't marry the girl. She's ready and willing."

They stopped in front of the hotel, the light from the lobby window falling across Rita's face, her amber hair red in the lamplight. Anger tugged at him and died. She was tired and a little cranky, and she had reason. He knew she had never really recovered from the sleep she had lost when she had sat up with him for so many nights.

"I'm not ready and willing," he said roughly.

He acted on impulse then, and taking her into his arms, brought her to him and kissed her. Afterwards he was never sure why he did it. She had not indicated she wanted his kiss, but her lips were sweet and clinging for a moment; her hands came up around his neck and were tight there. She drew back and looked at him, a sudden and unexpected tenderness in her eyes.

"That was wonderful," she said softly. Then the tenderness died. "But I guess you've had a lot of practice. I'm not one to steal another woman's man, Ben. Let's keep our minds on our business. I'm glad you're on your feet again. I think you'll have a job to do before long."

She whirled and went into the hotel. He stared after her, hearing the sharp tap of her heels as she crossed the lobby. She disappeared up the stairs and he went on toward his cabin, walking slowly, sourness piling up in him. He thought again, as he had so many times, that he was just a cog in her machine, another man who would help her do what she had set out to do, a man like Fred Purvane and John Meacham and the rest.

The next morning Sarboe left town with Zachary before sunup, riding south. For three days they worked every hole and riffle below the falls and their luck was good. Zachary swore at the end of the first day that he had never had so much fun, but by the end of the third day it had become plain labor with the fun gone out of it.

Through those three days Sarboe was too busy to think about his worries. Up here he could not hear the sawmill whistle; he could not hear the tall pines crashing to the ground and the fallers' yell, "Timber-r-r," or the banging of carpenters' hammers on River Street. He was away from the cursing of teamsters working on the ditch and the thunder of dynamite. For three days he was back in the silence of the wilderness just as he had been a few months before when he had received Mike Kelly's letter.

At night it was different. Lying beside the Deschutes with the campfire throwing a leaping red light across the small clearing and the whisper of the tumbling river in his ears, he had time to think and he found sleep evasive. It was beyond his understanding how so many lives could have jammed up together in this short time. He thought with some misgivings that they were woven into his own life. It was enough to feel that Rita's fortune depended upon him; it was too much to be forced to make decisions that would influence the lives of a dozen others.

Dallam's fat shadow fell upon them all. Sarboe had not seen the man since the day he had gone with Linda to talk to Kelly, but his presence was felt by everyone connected with Swift River. Nothing, or so he had been told, had been done to develop Dallam's town. Perhaps Dallam was waiting for railroad news. So far there had been nothing definite, but the country was filled with a dozen conflicting rumors. There could be only one other answer to Dallam's lack of aggressive action, his hope that Rita would go broke and he could buy the company's property at a bargain price.

Sarboe thought of Rita, wanting her and loving her and lacking any real hope that he would ever have her. She was too proud, too intent on her own destiny to look to any man for her happiness. Then he thought of Linda to whom he owed so much. She deserved the best and he could give her nothing.

Twice Holt Ricket had come for the mail since Cap had come that time, and both times Sarboe had seen Corey watching. He had a feeling. He was like a man helplessly watching a house burn down. Corey was the kind of man who was born for trouble, and Sarboe was not sure the Rickets were any different.

The fact that he might be imagining this connection between Shad Corey and the Rickets did not ease his mind. It only brought him back to George Dallam and a more logical explanation of Corey's presence in Swift River. In spite of his denial, he could well be Dallam's man, waiting until the sign was right to make a move that would match the thing Verd Ricket had tried to do. If this was true, it could in part at least explain Dallam's waiting.

They returned to Swift River the evening of the third, the big wagon loaded with trout varying in size from twelve inches on up to the big fellows over twenty. Neither Sarboe nor Zachary had kept count of the number they had caught. They could only hope they had enough.

It was dark when they rolled into town. The streets were crowded, and when Sarboe saw Lou Fain, he reined over to him, calling, "Get that bear, Lou?"

Fain shook a fat fist at Sarboe, shouting back, "You know damned well I can't go hunting in this altitude."

"Then I guess we'll all be eating trout tomorrow."

"We'll have bear steak, too," Fain yelled. "Purvane's boys fetched in two."

The Fourth was a day that Central Oregon would not forget soon. Meacham had done his job well. There were more than a thousand people in town: Dallam's ditch crew as well as Purvane's, businessmen looking for the rainbow's end, prospective settlers who had come in covered wagons from Burns across the desert, south from The Dalles, and eastward over the Santiam Pass from the Willamette Valley. It was a bigger crowd than Rita had expected, and she stayed in the townsite office from dawn until dark making the most of the opportunity.

It was a good day as far as the weather went, and a busy one for Sarboe as he had known it would be: stopping fights, patrolling the streets, and throwing drunks into his log jail to cool off. There were speeches by Lou Fain and John Meacham; there was a band that played most of the day, and dancing on the platform that had been erected near the river. Along with the rest of it, there were so many trout and bear steaks to eat that Lou Fain swore he'd have to diet for a month. He'd added twenty pounds trying to get his share, and Otis Barrett assured him he had succeeded.

Two things happened that gave Sarboe concern. First he had seen Linda and Shad Corey dancing; he saw the bright expression in Linda's dark eyes as she moved across the platform in Corey's arms. It was not a day, he thought, when he could step in and enforce his order. Corey must have sensed that, for he was challenging Sarboe by wearing his gun. When he saw Sarboe watching, he gave him a brittle stare, lips curling in a mirthless smile that was plainly defiant.

The second thing happened near evening when Corey, alone now, came to Sarboe as he moved through the crowd on River Street. He said, "Marshal, I've been wondering who thought this celebration up."

"Otis Barrett is running things," Sarboe said.

"Well, it's a hell of a day," Corey said in a complaining voice.

"You seem to be having a good time."

Corey shrugged. "Sure. Linda's the kind of woman I've been looking for all my life, and I don't figure you're man enough to hold two of 'em." He gave Sarboe his short grin, adding, "And I didn't figure you'd be telling me today what I could and couldn't do. That right?"

"I'll pass it up today," Sarboe said.

"You're being smart," Corey said approvingly.

"Maybe you'll be as smart tomorrow."

"No. Just today."

"Well now," Corey said, "that sounds like we might have some fun. I said I'd take them orders for a while. Remember?"

"You'll take 'em as long as you're in Swift River."

Corey's lips held no trace of a smile. His pale eyes raked Sarboe as he said, "We'll see as to that. Right now I've got an idea that's buzzing through my head like a bumblebee on the prod. Might liven this celebration up a little. Interested?"

"I doubt it."

"I'll tell you anyhow. Suppose we pull off a shooting contest, just you and me with a little side bet. Say, a thousand dollars."

Sarboe shook his head. "I haven't got that kind of money. Besides, I'm busy."

"Well then, fifty cents. I ain't particular."

"No."

"Make it for speed, Sarboe. I've been wondering how fast you were. We'll start with guns in our holsters. Shoot five times. A tin can will do for a target. Just keep it moving. Or maybe you're afraid, Marshal."

"No, not afraid," Sarboe said evenly. "Just too busy," and turned away.

Sarboe puzzled over Corey's challenge the rest of the day, uncertain what motive lay behind it. It might have stemmed from his confidence in his own gun skill, or perhaps from a boyish desire to show off before Linda.

After it was dark there was a display of fireworks over the river, another three hours before Swift River quieted down and Sarboe with a clear conscience could walk wearily along the now silent and littered Main Street to his cabin. There he found Holt Ricket waiting for him.

"Came for the mail," Holt said.

Sarboe lighted a lamp. He looked in the rack and shook his head. "Nothing here, Holt." He stepped outside and noticed that young Ricket was standing at the corner of the cabin so that the lamplight did not touch him. Sarboe asked, "It's been quite a day. Why didn't you and Cap come in for the fun?"

"We worked," Holt said sulkily. "We ain't got time for foolishment."

He disappeared and presently Sarboe heard him riding away. Sarboe went to bed, wondering why Holt had come tonight. He had been here a week before and there had seldom been any mail important enough to warrant a ride to town.

The Rickets lived a lonely life that wasn't natural for a man as young as Holt. Perhaps he had been waiting there in the darkness, listening to the music and watching the fireworks. It was possible that Cap hadn't allowed him to come for the day, and Holt had promised to watch from a distance, taking this small pleasure from a day that had been a cause of celebration for a thousand other men.

Bone weary, Sarboe went to sleep. It seemed only a few minutes later that a banging on his door woke him, but it had been several hours, for the sun was showing in the east. He pulled on his pants, calling, "All right, I'm coming." When he opened the door, he saw that it was the water man, Curly Hewitt, who stood there, trembling, a worried and frightened man.

"Got a corpse out here." Hewitt took off his hat and wiped his bald head. "You know I go up river above the sawmill to get water. My barrels was plumb empty, and I knowed folks would need some water right away, so I pulled out of town afore sunup. I found this hombre in the road 'bout a mile south of town. Shot in the back, looks like."

Sarboe pushed past him and strode to the wagon. A dead man lay in the wagon beside the empty water barrels. It was Holt Ricket. Sarboe reached down and lifted a cold hand. Holt had been dead for several hours.

Chapter XV

THE BURIAL

THE sun was laying a hard brittle glare upon the desert when Sarboe topped the ridge above the Ricket ranch and rode down the rocky slope toward the big stone house. Cap's horse in the corral back of the barn was the only sign of life about the place.

All the way out from Swift River Sarboe had been trying to think of a way to tell Cap about Holt. Now, reining up in front of the house, Sarboe knew there was no substitute for the brutal truth at such a time. He stepped down and tied, and when he started toward the house, he saw that Cap was standing in the doorway, his long back very straight, his black beard carefully combed.

Cap stood motionless, giving Sarboe no greeting. He was wearing a clean shirt and brown broadcloth pants that looked as if they had just been pressed; his boots had been recently polished. His long black hair was brushed down flat against his head and trimmed a little along the back; his dark eyes were fixed on Sarboe's face, as brightly brittle as two pieces of chipped obsidian in the sunlight. Sarboe stopped ten feet from the doorway, staring up at the big man, and he thought, *He knows.*

For a moment neither said anything, Cap waiting, Sarboe wondering how he could have heard. Then Sarboe said, "Holt was shot and killed sometime last night."

Cap gave a short nod, holding that same expressionless mask upon his dark face. Sarboe said, "You heard?"

"No, but I knew. He'd have been back if he hadn't been killed. He wanted to go to town yesterday and I wouldn't let him. About dusk he saddled up and rode out. Didn't say a word about where he was going. Wanted to see the fireworks, I reckon."

Cap walked past Sarboe toward the barn. Puzzled, Sarboe fell into step with him. He had never understood the Rickets and he didn't understand Cap now. He said, "I sent a man over to Dallamville to tell Verd if he was there. I figured if he wasn't, Dallam or Kelly would know where he was."

"I don't reckon Verd will come. He don't give a damn about nobody, Verd don't."

Cap went into the barn. He took a knife out of his pocket and picking up a wagon tailboard that was leaning against the wall, began to carve letters across one end. There was silence a moment, Cap's sharp-pointed knife slicing deeply into the weathered wood. Then he asked, "Where's the body?"

"It's coming in a wagon. I rode on ahead, figuring you'd want to know."

"Thanks." Cap kept on carving, and presently he said, "Tell me about it.'

Sarboe told him about Holt's asking for the mail and about Curly Hewitt's finding the body. Then he added, "I went over to the spot where Curly found him, but I didn't turn up a damned thing."

"You said he was shot in the back?"

Sarboe nodded. "It was a clear night. Lot of stars and part of a moon. A man could have ridden alongside the road and let him have it after he went by, but I sure couldn't cut no sign."

"Who done it?"

"I figured you'd have more of a notion on that than I would."

"How would I know anything about it?"

"Ever hear of a man named Shad Corey?"

Cap shook his head. "I know some Shadwells. Their mother's name was Corey. I reckon one of 'em might be this Shad Corey."

"You knew he was in town?"

"No, but I ain't surprised. I figured we'd be warned,

but we wasn't. Verd said we couldn't trust nobody. That's the only thing I ever knew Verd to be right about."

"I'd better get back to town and pick Corey up."

"Ain't got nothing to hold him on, have you?"

"No."

Cap raised his eyes to Sarboe's face. He said hesitantly, "I'd like it if you'd stay. Don't seem right for me to be the only one here when I bury him."

"If you know something about Corey, I might be able to make him talk."

"Shadwells don't talk. What does this Corey look like?"

Sarboe described him and Cap nodded. "That's Ty Shadwell. He's the youngest one of the boys." He laid down the tailboard and pocketed his knife. "You'll stay?"

Sarboe hesitated. "Corey might light out . . ."

"You said you didn't have nothing to hold him on. Besides, he'll stay in the country till he gets me and Verd. Be a good thing for you if he does get Verd." Cap picked up a shovel. "You wouldn't know, Holt not being one to talk much, but he looked up to you. After you licked Verd, he said he wished he was as good a man as you were. It'd be fitting if you'd help me bury him."

"All right," Sarboe said. "I'll stay."

"I'd be beholden to you." Cap handed Sarboe the shovel. "I've got another one back of the house."

Sarboe waited in the shade of the barn, thinking of the time he had tangled with Verd here in front of the house and Holt had said, "He just likes to fight. Fighting's like whiskey is to some men. He'll try you again one of these days." And he thought of the warning Holt had given him in Swift River. "You watch out for him. He ain't gonna rest till he gets you."

Strange men, these Rickets, and nothing Cap had said helped Sarboe to understand them. There must have been a deep and passionate hatred between Verd and Holt, and whatever admiration Holt had felt for Sarboe must have stemmed from the inner knowledge of his own weakness, his inability to do the thing Sarboe had done.

No hatred was quite as feral as that between two brothers. Sarboe had seen a few examples of it. Now, watching Cap come toward the barn with the other shovel, it struck Sarboe that this bitterness between the two boys might partially at least explain the strange way the Rickets lived.

"We'll bury him above the house," Cap said. "He was the only one of us who liked it here. Always claimed it was a pretty view." He shook his head. "Me, I don't see anything pretty in it. Fact is, I haven't seen anything pretty since we left New Mexico."

Cap picked up the tailboard and they walked past the barn and on up the ridge until they reached a spot that suited Cap. He dropped the tailboard and paced off the grave. He said, "I'll put a fence around come morning. Then I'll be moving out. Nothing to hold me here now."

"You can't walk off and leave your outfit," Sarboe said.

Cap straightened, eyes turning to the stone house. "I'll round up my cattle and sell 'em to you for whatever you want to pay. If anybody wants to live here, they can. I built that house stout, thinking it'd keep Holt from being afraid, but nothing could do that."

Cap started to dig, motioning for Sarboe to take the other end. It was sandy soil, loose and dry, and kept trickling back into the grave. Before they were six feet down they struck a solid ledge of rock. Cap climbed out and threw down his shovel. "It'll have to do."

"Got a coffin?"

Cap shook his head. "We'll roll him up in a canvas. Won't make no difference to Holt. He won't feel the cold now, or the snow and rain. He won't feel nothing and maybe it's for the best." He wiped a sleeve across his forehead, staring at the grave. "You wouldn't know how it's been with me, Sarboe, having a feeling this was bound to come and not knowing how to stop it.''

They walked down the slope, Cap looking out across the broad sweep of sand and sagebrush and rimrock. He said bitterly, ''My wife died when Holt was born. Maybe she could have done something with Verd if she'd lived. I dunno. All I know is I've been the damnedest failure a father could be. I thought I had to keep my boys together, but that was the biggest mistake I ever made.''

When they reached the house, Cap said, ''I'll fix something to eat. Go take care of your horse. Might be quite a while before the body gets here.''

Cap crossed the barren yard to the back door. Sarboe turned toward his horse, loosend the cinch, and watered him. He put him into the back stall of the barn, and forked hay into the manger, beginning now to understand Holt. Sensitive, wanting peace and beauty, he had been lost in a world that held neither. Probably he had been afraid of Verd when they were kids, and Verd, like a mean dog, had worked on that fear.

When Sarboe reached the kitchen, he saw that Cap had a fire going and had placed a coffeepot on the front of the stove. He fried bacon, opened a can of tomatoes and emptied it into a dish, and set a plate of cold biscuits on the table. Then, as they ate, he talked, apparently welcoming the opportunity.

''We had a good spread in New Mexico,'' Cap said. ''East of Las Vegas a piece. Before the boys got big enough to work, I had to leave 'em home a lot. I had a Mexican woman keeping house for a while. Verd was ornery even then. Born that way, I reckon. He licked Holt about once a day. I used a black snake on him, but it never done no good. Then we had hard times. You'll remember how it was 'bout '93. Verd was big enough to ride with me and I had to let the woman go. I made Holt stay home and do the cooking for us. That gave Verd a chance to hooraw Holt about being a girl.''

Cap rose and filled the coffee cups, black eyes somber with the memories. He sat down and stirred his coffee, staring at it as if he didn't see it. "All the time I kept thinking it would work out when the boys got older and I could get a woman back to keep house, but things got worse. We had trouble with the Shadwells. They had a spread next to ours and I reckon they rustled a few of our steers. I couldn't prove nothing and neither could the sheriff, but Verd kept saying that was what they was doing. One day he beat one of the Shadwell boys so bad he damned near died."

Cap drank his coffee and, setting the cup down, wiped the back of his hand across his mouth. "I didn't know it, but Verd kept hammering at Holt about being yellow. He was, I reckon, but I ain't blaming him. He just wasn't made for fighting like Verd was, but it finally got so Holt couldn't stand it. One day in town he drilled old man Shadwell in the back. We lit out. Didn't have no choice. We got over Raton Pass into Colorado and I hid Holt out. I went back and sneaked into town at night.

"Well, I sold everything I had to a gent I thought was a friend of mine. Took a big loss but it was the best I could do. I told this fellow I'd let him know where we were and made him promise to write to me if one of the Shadwells took after us. That's why we wanted our mail, but we never heard from this fellow. I reckon he finally told young Shadwell where we was."

"Might have been an accident that he landed up here," Sarboe said.

"Too big a country. But that's why we didn't like it when you told us Kelly had this irrigation notion. We settled here because it was empty country. We figured if a boom started somebody might drift in who knew us. Anyhow, living here by ourselves didn't work. Holt never got over killing old man Shadwell. Verd hoorawed him so much he went kind of loco. Got so he couldn't sleep. I told Verd I'd kill him if he didn't let Holt alone. I reckon I'm the only man on this earth Verd was ever afraid of, but shutting him up didn't do no good. Holt was scared of his own shadow. Couldn't even go to Prineville and get drunk enough to have any fun.''

Cap rose and walked to the window. He said, his back to Sarboe, "You wouldn't savvy the hell I've been living in. I thought if I could hold the boys together, they'd get to thinking of each other like brothers ought to, but it just got worse. After Verd had that fight with you and came crawling home, I told him that if he left again he didn't need to come back. I told him you was just a better man and to forget about getting square, but he won't, Sarboe. You'll have to kill him or be killed. It's written in the book that way.''

Outside a man called, "Hello the house."

Sarboe rose. "Holt's body's here, Cap."

Cap took a long, ragged breath. "You go out, Sarboe. Leave the body in the barn and send the fellow back to town."

Sarboe left the house, motioning for the man in the wagon to drive to the barn. They lifted the body to the ground. Sarboe said, "You go on back, Carl. No need to stay for the burying."

The driver nodded and, stepping back into the wagon seat, drove away. Cap remained in the house until the wagon had dropped over the ridge, then he came across the yard, a worn *Bible* in his hand. He knelt beside Holt's body and lifted the sheet that covered his face. For a long moment he remained there, staring at his son's thin stiff face, then he rose and, bringing a piece of canvas from the barn, spread it on the ground. Sarboe helped him roll the body into it. He handed the *Bible* to Sarboe and, stooping, lifted Holt and trudged up the slope to the grave.

"I'll help . . ." Sarboe began.

"No," Cap said.

Cap was breathing hard by the time they reached the grave. He laid the body inside it and took the *Bible* from Sarboe. He stood motionless, eyes lifted to the sky as if

he were praying, then he opened the *Bible*. He had placed
a marker at the *Twenty-third Psalm*. He read it laboriously as if each word was an effort for him. Then he
laid the *Bible* beside a clump of sagebrush and moved
to Holt's head. Sarboe took his feet and they lowered
the body into the grave.

Cap picked up a shovel and began filling the grave,
head lowered. Sarboe could not see his face, but he felt
the intensity of emotion that was in the man. Not in
anything he said, nor was there any expression on his
dark, inscrutable face that indicated his feelings, but it
was there.

Sarboe took the other shovel and when the sandy soil
filled the grave and was shaped in a long mound over
it, Cap took the tailboard and shoved one end into the
loose soil. He had carved, HOLT RICKET GONE TO
ETERNAL PEACE. He busied himself for a moment
picking up pieces of lava rock and placing them around
the base of the tailboard, then he picked up the shovels
and strode back down the slope.

Cap walked rapidly in long strides, eyes lifted to the
sky, and Sarboe had to run to keep up with him. He said
nothing until they reached the barn. Then he laid the
shovels down and turned to face Sarboe, and for the first
time Sarboe saw that there were tears in his black eyes.
He brushed the back of his hand across his eyes, blinking a little as he said, "Must have got some of that
damned sand in my eyes. It's a hell of a country, Sarboe. I'm getting out."

"Why don't you come to Swift River?" Sarboe asked.
"I'll give you a job if you want to work for me. You
haven't got anywhere to go, have you?"

"No," Cap said, "but I reckon I'd better just drift
along. Thank you kindly, Sarboe. It ain't easy for me
to ask for help like I done today, but I needed some."

"I was glad . . ." Sarboe stopped. Verd had ridden
up and was dismounting.

Sarboe glanced at Cap's bleak face and then turned his head to watch Verd who had seen them and was coming toward the barn. Sarboe eased his gun in leather, wanting no trouble but not knowing how it could be avoided if Verd wanted to push. There was bound to be a final settlement between him and Verd. As Cap had said, it was written in the book that way, but the day of Holt's burial was not the time for it.

"You can stop right there," Cap called. "Holt's buried. Get back on your horse and ride."

Still Verd came on, head thrust forward on his great shoulders, knobby face showing scars that Sarboe's fists had put upon it. He did not stop until he was twenty feet away, then he motioned toward Sarboe. He said, his voice ugly, "What the hell's he doing here?"

"Get out," Cap roared. "I told you not to come back . . ."

"It was my brother you buried. You should have waited for me."

"Your brother," Cap said scornfully. "Took you a hell of a long time to find that out. Damn the day you was ever conceived. Damn your mother and me for . . ."

"He killed Holt." Verd motioned again toward Sarboe. "Now you take him in like he was a son."

"You're crazy. It was Ty Shadwell that done it." Cap's hands fisted at his sides. "I wish Sarboe was my son. I wish to hell he was. I could have some pride in me instead of shame. Get out of the country, Verd. Keep riding till you're a thousand miles away."

"I said he killed Holt. Don't you believe me?"

"No, I don't believe you. I'd come nearer believing you done it. Get out now, I tell you."

Verd stood motionless, glittering eyes pinned on Sarboe. He said, "No, I reckon you wouldn't believe me."

"You don't really believe it yourself, do you?" Sarboe asked.

"Believing and proving are two different things," Verd said hoarsely. "I ain't leaving the country. Not till you're finished, Sarboe."

"Maybe you'd better do the finishing yourself," Sarboe said softly. "Today."

"Not today, but the day's coming when I will, and it's coming pretty damned soon. You'll be finished along with that Gentry woman and George Dallam will be the big gun on this range." Verd tapped his barrel-like chest. "I'm the man to do it. It won't be that loud-talking Mike Kelly. It'll be me and don't you forget it."

"Haven't you made enough trouble?" Cap cried.

"Trouble? Hell, I ain't got started yet."

"Then I'll stop you," Cap shouted passionately. "So help me, I'll stop you."

Verd threw back his great head and laughed. "You've whupped me for the last time. I used to be scared of you a little, but I ain't now. George Dallam is my kind of man. I wish I'd known him before. He's going to the top and I'm going along. Stay out of my way, old man."

Wheeling, Verd stalked back to his horse and, mounting, rode over the ridge. Sarboe watched him go until he was out of sight. Verd, he thought, did not have the kind of sand in his craw that he wanted everyone to believe, not the kind of sand that would let him face a man and draw his gun, but he was all the more dangerous because of that weakness.

"I'm sorry," Cap said bitterly. "I told you how it was."

"Don't blame yourself."

"Who else can I blame?" Cap demanded. "If there is a hell, I reckon Verd'll be punished for his sins and Holt's, too."

"Is there anything else I can do for you?"

"No. You'd best be riding now. Maybe I'll take that job, Sarboe. I'll take it till Verd's dead."

Sarboe turned into the runway and walked toward his horse. He tightened the cinch and backed his horse out of the stall. Cap, watching him, said, "Sarboe, I ain't been a religious man. Maybe not a good one, neither, failing like I've done with Verd. This here *Bible* was my wife's. Today's the first time I've opened it since she died." He drew in a long breath. "Took me a hell of a long time to even find that psalm."

Cap was silent for moment, standing there looking at Sarboe as if there was something else he wanted to say. Then he said, his voice begging for assurance, "Tell me one thing, Sarboe. Tell me what I wrote on the tailboard was right. Holt is at peace now, ain't he? He never done anything wrong but drill old man Shadwell, and Verd was to blame for that. The Lord won't hold it against Holt, will He?"

If it had been another time and another man asking the question, Sarboe would have said he didn't know anything about such matters, but he sensed the agony that was in Cap Ricket, the self-condemnation that would be in him as long as he lived, so he said as if he were certain, "No, the Lord won't hold it against Holt. He's at peace all right."

A light seemed to break across Cap's face. He said eagerly, "I've got to believe that, Sarboe. I've got to."

Chapter XVI

ULTIMATUM

SARBOE rode westward, the sun dipping down toward the high Cascades and throwing a brief scarlet stain upon the snow peaks. Clouds lay along the mountain tops, and they, too, were touched by the spreading glory of the sunset. Then it changed, quite suddenly as it did almost every night now, for the sun had dropped behind the peaks and purple shadow flowed out across the juniper forest and the ragged buttes and rocky crests that made up this land between the mountains and the desert.

Sarboe had never tired of the nightly display of changing color, the deepening purple cloak that blotted out the ridge lines until the sky and the land seemed to flow together, but tonight he was hardly aware of it, nor was he aware of the coolness that came with the sunset. A worry had settled upon him, a strange uneasiness that he seldom felt. What Verd had said about his being finished was responsible for it. Not that he was afraid of Verd. Rather it was the uncertainty of time and knowledge of the move Dallam would make.

He had thought that Verd had gone to work for George Dallam because he wanted to be on the side of anyone who was against Ben Sarboe. Now Sarboe sensed there was more to it than that. Verd wanted to be big and he saw a chance to grow with Dallam. It meant, Sarboe thought, that Dallam had found in Verd the tool he wanted. He had probably thought Mike Kelly would do, but Mike was strong on talking and weak on doing. Verd was the opposite, and that would suit Dallam.

Sarboe had not seen Mike for a long time, and he wondered now if Mike realized he would be thrown overboard when the time suited Dallam. Mike was smart enough; it was a case of his coming to grips with reality. Linda would never again compromise with him. He must know that, and in the end Linda's defiance might balance off Mike's faith in his grandiose dreams.

By the time the lights of Swift River showed through the pines, Sarboe's thoughts had come to Rita as they always did sooner or later. Cap Ricket's life had been bound to his sons' lives; Linda's was bound to Mike's, but Rita had no more family than Sarboe did. She had come to live within herself, to take an inordinate pride in her accomplishments in what she liked to call "a man's world." She would not change as long as that pride drove her as it did now, but unless she changed, Sarboe could have no real hope in ever holding her love.

Sarboe came to the road a little south of his cabin and turned toward the town. He had some questions to ask Corey if the man was still around, but he had a feeling that Shad Corey would be hard to find. He was not convinced that Cap had been right in saying Corey would stay until he had killed all the Rickets, Holt was the one who had murdered old man Shadwell, Cap had said, so it was likely that Corey would consider his job done with Holt's murder.

Sarboe rode past his cabin and went on to the business block, dark now except for the light in the hotel and the townsite office. Rita, Sarboe thought, was working overtime again. The bookkeeper she had sent for had not come. Sarboe reined up in front of the hotel, dismounted and tied, and went in.

Abe Tottle was at the desk, and an expression of relief broke across his face the instant he saw Sarboe. "Mister, I'm glad to see you," Tottle cried. "Rita wants you to get over to the office pronto."

"In a minute," Sarboe said. "I'm looking for Shad Corey."

"Haven't seen him for quite a spell," Tottle said. "I just took the desk half an hour ago. He might be up in his room if he ain't over on River Street."

"I'll take a look in his room."

"No," Tottle said sharply. "You get over to the office. Dallam and Kelly rode in a little while ago. Rita needs you."

Sarboe stiffened, thinking again that Verd had said it would not be long until Sarboe and Rita were finished. Dallam's and Kelly's presence in Swift River was the last thing Sarboe expected. There could be only one explanation. Dallam had decided to play his high trump, and he was letting Rita see his card before he made the play, hoping to force some sort of a compromise.

Wheeling, Sarboe left the hotel on the run. The door of the townsite office was open, lamplight falling through it and across the boardwalk in a long, yellow splash. Sarboe stepped into the light and went on through the door, breathing hard. Rita was sitting back of her desk, her face as pale as Sarboe had ever seen it. Dallam stood across the desk from her, soft hands folded in front of him, his pink-cheeked face very innocent. Kelly stood behind him and to one side, staring morosely at the floor as if this was not to his liking.

Dallam was talking, but he stopped when he heard Sarboe come in and looked around. Rita turned her head, and when she saw Sarboe, she half rose, then quickly dropped back. She breathed, "Ben, where have you been?"

"At Ricket's place." Sarboe moved toward Dallam. "What in hell are you doing here?"

Dallam's expression remained unchanged. "Getting tough won't help you or Miss Gentry. I came here in peace and I hold no ill will to anyone. There is only one way to settle trouble, and I have come to suggest that way."

Sarboe glanced at Kelly. He said, "Howdy Mike. Have you seen Linda?"

Kelly's gaze brushed Sarboe's face and was lowered again. He said, "No."

Mike Kelly had the look of a beaten man. He was a follower now, not a leader, and it showed in his freckled face. The old lustiness was gone from him; no glib words came rolling easily off his tongue as they usually did.

"It's been quite a while since you saw her, Mike," Sarboe said.

There was a silence for a time, then Dallam said, "We are not here to see Linda. I have no sympathy for anyone who picks the weak side."

Sarboe grinned derisively. "So you think Linda picked the weak side. That sounds funny, coming from you."

Dallam grinned back. He said, "No, not funny. Make no mistake on that point, my friend, and don't get wisdom mixed up with weakness. I have always been proud of my wisdom Sarboe. For instance, I peg Purvane as a smart engineer. He's dug a good ditch. Now I want it."

"I don't blame you for wanting it," Sarboe said. "Want me to throw 'em out, Rita?"

"The hell with 'em," Kelly shouted. "I told you, George. Let's ride."

"Wait a minute." Rita threw out a protesting hand. "Dallam has a proposition. I want you to hear it, Ben."

Pleased, Dallam said, "All right, but first, Sarboe, I must remind you that we have a moral right to this townsite. If this should go to court, our moral right is important. A man of your caliber never understands that."

"Your proposition?"

"I'm getting to it. I want to explain one more thing. We have not made any trouble since Verd Ricket's fiasco. Now I'll tell you the reason. It suited our purpose for Purvane to go ahead. When we first came, I planned to make things so tough that you'd quit. Then I learned something that changed my mind." Dallam flicked a bit of dust from his sleeve. "I have connections with important people. Railroad men. Politicians. Bankers. In this case it was a banker. I was informed that Miss Gentry's finances were too meager to carry this project through."

"He's lying, ain't he, Rita?" Sarboe demanded.

Rita was staring at her desk top, a finger idly tracing a pattern on its smooth surface. She said, "Let him talk, Ben."

Dallam laughed softly. "She's not denying it, friend. You know why? It's true. I keep myself informed on things like that. We have started a ditch, a small one, I admit, but it will do for my purpose. From the first I aimed to use yours to get water on my land."

Dallam moved back to sit down on Sarboe's desk, his hands still folded across his round belly. "The tough part of the work has been done. That's why I aim to take over shortly. From here on the water can be turned into natural channels. The flume has been built on a sharp grade with a capacity of one hundred and sixty cubic feet a second. It will reclaim twenty thousand acres and that's the size of my segregation."

"How would he know that if Linda hadn't told him?" Rita demanded. "I said she was a spy."

"She isn't any such thing," Kelly shouted. "She hasn't told us anything."

"She wouldn't know them figures," Sarboe said.

"My source of information is unimportant," Dallam said. "Your man Meacham has done a fine job with his newspaper. By fall the settlers will be pouring in by the hundreds, but they will settle on my segregation, not yours. You wasted money on that big four-wheeled scraper." He snorted. "Takes four teams to pull it, but I'll buy it along with the rest of your equipment. I can afford it. I have money of my own and I've sold shares of stock. What's more, I have backing from capitalists who know a good investment when they see it."

Sarboe looked at Rita, but he saw no assurance on her worried face. He glanced at Kelly, then at Dallam. He said, "George, I've heard some big windies come out of Mike, but I'm surprised at you."

"This is no windy, Sarboe. I came here to buy you and Miss Gentry out, lock, stock, and barrel. Townsite included. If you agree I'll make out your check now."

"How much?" Sarboe demanded.

"I'll take Miss Gentry's word for her expenses, and I'll give you twenty-five cents on the dollar."

"Why, you chiseling, two-bit tinhorn," Sarboe breathed. "Get out."

"You've got twelve hours to think it over," Dallam said coolly. "Remember I'm not Mike Kelly. You two have underestimated me from the first."

"Suppose we don't take it?" Rita asked.

"Things will begin to happen," Dallam said. "I'm not threatening. I'm telling you. As I said before, there is one way to avoid trouble. I'd rather put out a little money and take everything over than be forced to destroy something I can use later. If you refuse to save what you can, you'll wind up with nothing."

"Then that's where we'll wind up," Sarboe said hotly, "and you're making a mistake if you're figuring on Verd Ricket's playing hell for you. I can still take care of Verd."

"Not this time, friend." Dallam jerked his head at the door. "Come on, Mike. Twelve hours will be enough for them to see the light."

Dallam moved to the door, Kelly following. Sarboe said, "Mike, there's something here that smells worse than you're seeing."

"You don't see a smell, Sarboe," Dallam murmured, "and if Mike don't smell it, the smell isn't there."

"It's there, all right. Mike, listen to me. The first time I talked to Linda, she said you had more ambition than talent. This sure as hell proves it. Can't you see where you're coming out?"

"I'm not coming," Kelly said bitterly. "I've got my eyes open but that doesn't mean I'm quitting George. I'm just working for him now."

Kelly went out of the office then. Dallam lingered, the corners of his mouth holding a confident smile. "Twelve hours, Miss Gentry." Then he followed Kelly, and a moment later Sarboe heard the mutter of hoofs as they left town.

Sarboe swung back to face Rita. He said, "I've never asked you about money, but I figured you were too smart to play it close. How about it?"

"I'm broke." She lifted her head and met his gaze. "Go on. Tell me I'm seven kinds of a fool, but I'm still broke. I didn't even send for that bookkeeper. I couldn't afford his salary when I could do the work. Maybe I've been crazy, buying machinery like the big scraper, but I kept thinking I could sell enough lots to keep the work going on the ditch." She spread her hands. "It's no good, Ben. I can't even meet the next payroll. Dallam made a good guess. He's been waiting until the sign was right and he hit it."

Sarboe came around the desk and, taking her hands, brought her to her feet. "We're not taking Dallam's offer. If we go down, we go down." Then he stopped and shook his head, for it struck him that this was not for him to say. "It's your investment. Not mine. Do what you have to do."

"Ben, Ben." She blinked, the corners of her mouth working. "I don't want to deal with Dallam. If it was just me, I'd rather go broke. You know that, but I've brought these men in, John Meacham and Abe Tottle and the rest. I've always been in little deals before, but this is big. I just didn't realize how money melts when you're up against construction like this. Fred knew how it was going, but I kept holding him off. I was counting on doing a lot of business with the men who were here for the Fourth, but most of them were just looking."

"If we had a few weeks . . ."

"We don't, Ben. That's just it. We've got to pay men to keep them on the job and we've got to feed them. We've got to have the main ditch finished and some laterals dug when the settlers begin coming in."

"I'll get Ricket's beef. We can stall him, and we'll get a loan from Otis Barrett to meet the payroll."

She drew her hands away from him and walked toward the door. "Blow the lamp out, Ben."

He obeyed and followed her, feeling the sense of utter failure that was weighing so heavily upon her. She locked the door, and he turned toward the hotel with her. He said, "Rita, it's your damned fool pride that keeps you from going to Barrett. It just ain't smart."

"Dad used to tell me my pride would ruin me," she said, "and maybe it will, but I can't help it. These men trust me. I told them I wouldn't need their financial help when I asked them to come to the Deschutes. Don't you see how I'd feel, asking for a loan now?''

''How will they feel when you sell out to Dallam?''

''They own their lots and they have their businesses going. No matter who owns the townsite, they'll get along.''

''But a thieving pirate like Dallam . . .''

''I know, Ben, but in the end he'll pull out. Somebody else will take the project and it will be finished. We've started honestly and in the end it will be honest. It seems awfully important to me to get it finished.''

They had reached the hotel then and she turned to him, her head tilted back, the lamplight touching her face. She was not the same proud Rita; she seemed very tired. The weight of these weeks had been too much for her.

''I'll see you in the morning,'' Sarboe said.

Turning, he walked toward his horse and mounted. She was still standing there when he rode away, and it was not until he was in bed that he remembered Shad Corey.

Chapter XVII

THE SELLOUT

SARBOE woke at dawn. He rose at once, thinking that this was probably the day. Destiny had taken a dozen lives and woven a pattern to suit its own taste. Because Sarboe's life was one of the dozen, he felt himself bound in with the others. The weaving would soon be finished. Today. Or tomorrow. Or the next day. But it would be soon just as Verd Ricket had said so confidently.

The question in Sarboe's mind now was how much he could interfere. He had agreed to let Rita handle the business end and he would handle the trouble. She had not been entirely satisfied to let it go at that, but when he insisted on something, Rita had not made an issue out of it. If he went to Otis Barrett now, he would be interfering with Rita's half of the bargain.

By the time Sarboe had cooked breakfast and eaten, he had made up his mind. He'd go to Barrett whether Rita liked it or not. He had no idea how big a loan would be necessary, or whether Barrett had enough money to do the job, but the least the banker could do would be to string along even if it meant he'd end up as broke as Rita. Making any kind of a deal with Dallam was out of the question, and it was hard to believe that Rita would even consider it.

Sarboe stacked his dishes on the table and, leaving them there, fed and watered his horse. He went first to the hotel, thinking it would be better to wait for Barrett to come down to the bank. The night clerk was still at the desk, and when Sarboe asked about Corey, he shook his head.

"I haven't seen him, Marshal," the clerk said. "He might be in his room. His key isn't here."

"What room?"

"Eighteen, but I don't think you'd better . . ."

"You trying to get in the way of the law?"

The clerk shrugged. "Not me, Marshal. Go ahead and bust his door down."

Sarboe climbed the stairs and turned down the hall until he came to Corey's room. He knocked on the door, but there was no answer. He tried the knob. The door was unlocked and swung open. No one was there, the bed had not been slept in, and none of Corey's things were around. Sarboe stood there a moment, swearing softly. Corey had made a run for it, satisfied with murdering Holt. By this time he could be fifty miles away in an empty, trackless country.

Sarboe went back down the stairs and into the street, torn between two demands. He should let the sheriff in

Prineville know. He considered the direction Corey would be most likely to take. He wouldn't go east. It was too far across the high desert to Burns, especially for a man who did not know the country. Probably not north, for there were some ranches along the road, stagecoaches were running between Swift River and Shaniko, and there would be any number of freight outfits and settler wagons coming south. Corey would not want to be seen until he had put a good many miles between him and Swift River.

Sarboe lingered on the boardwalk, smoking and watching the town come to life. He had been both the hunter and the hunted, and he understood how the mind of a fugitive worked. Corey would travel fast; he would avoid ranches and towns until necessity drove him to other humans for food. If he went west, he would cross the Santiam Pass and come to the Willamette Valley which was the most thickly settled part of the state, and he could not avoid meeting people on the road for the pass was well traveled during the summer.

South? Sarboe finished his cigarette, deciding that it was Corey's most logical route. He might go to Klamath Falls or he could turn southeast to Silver Lake and go on to Lakeview. There were a few scattered ranches, but he could avoid them, and it was not likely he would meet many people on the road, perhaps no one if he dodged the stage.

If Sarboe were in Corey's shoes, that was the route he would take. Finding him would be like hunting for the proverbial needle in the haystack, but he had to try. He turned back into the lobby asking, "Did Corey pay his bill?"

The clerk shook his head. "He owes us for a month's room rent."

Sarboe nodded and left the hotel. It was enough to bring Corey back for. Once he had the man in jail, he'd find a way to make him talk. Cap Ricket had assured him a Shadwell would not talk, but this was one who would. Sarboe would have no conscience about the method he used, not when he was dealing with the man who had shot Holt Ricket in the back.

Sarboe glanced at his watch. It would be more than an hour before Barrett would be in the bank and Sarboe could not afford to waste an hour. He swung up a short side street that led to Barrett's house and knocked. The banker opened the door and stood there, barring Sarboe's entrance and staring uneasily at him as if afraid of what he was going to say.

"Howdy," Sarboe said.

"Morning, Ben," the banker said coldly, still making no move to invite him in.

Breakfast smells came to Sarboe. He saw Mrs. Barrett standing at the stove, her back to him, and suddenly it struck Sarboe that there was something wrong about this. Barrett's thin, sandy hair was brushed down over his forehead; his small, puckered mouth had the appearance of a tightly drawn purse. He seemed neither friendly nor hostile as he waited for Sarboe to state his business.

Sarboe did not know the man well, not in the way he knew Doc Zachary and Lou Fain, and he didn't like him as well as he did the others, although Barrett had always been friendly enough in a cool, restrained way. Now he stood as if frozen in the doorway, the only show of life the blinking of his eyes and the slow movement of his teeth as he chewed on a mouthful of breakfast.

Because he was pressed by the shortage of time, Sarboe blurted, "Rita's broke, Otis."

"I know," Barrett said.

"How did you know?"

"I'm her banker. I've tried to talk to her about her financial affairs, but you know Rita."

"We need a loan."

"The bank can't give you one," Barrett said quickly. "You might as well get this straight, Ben. At the present time your company is not a good risk. Not for any bank."

Sarboe stared at the little man, finding it hard to believe he had heard right. "When we fixed up the board of trade, you said . . ."

"That was a good many weeks ago. Rita could have sold some stock, enough to give her sufficient working capital, but she's so damned stubborn she had to have her way." He spread his hands as if he considered her case hopeless. "Now it's too late."

It began making sense. Sarboe had wondered how Dallam had found out about Rita's financial trouble. He had assumed that some banker in Portland or The Dalles had known how much Rita had when she'd come to Swift River and had told Dallam. Now it struck him that Otis Barrett was the informer. It was hard to accept that, for Rita had faith in the men she had brought to the Deschutes, but it must be that way.

Sarboe said softly, "It's not too late, Otis. Purvane has built a good ditch, hasn't he?"

Barrett nodded. "Yes. Fred's a good engineer."

"What's the capacity of the flume he's been building?"

"One hundred and sixty cubic feet a second. Why?"

"I'll tell you," Sarboe shouted, self-control leaving him. He grabbed a handful of the banker's shirt and shook him. "You're selling Rita out. You're a bigger damned crook than Dallam ever was. You told him Rita was flat on her back and you told him about the ditch." He shook the banker again. "Dallam was here last night trying to buy us out. He wouldn't have had the figures on the flume and he wouldn't have known Rita was broke if you hadn't told him."

"I didn't do nothing of the kind," Barrett squalled. "Let go."

Releasing his grip, Sarboe struck Barrett on the side of the head. The banker sprawled back into the room as his wife grabbed a frying pan off the stove and whirled, brandishing the pan above her head. She screamed, "Get out of here. Get out now and leave Otis alone."

But Sarboe didn't move. He stared down at Barrett, hating him. He said, "I want the truth, Otis."

"All right. I told Dallam." Barrett sat up and brought a hand across his face. "I've got to save my bank and I can't save it by backing a fool woman like Rita. She wouldn't listen to me or Purvane or anybody. Now if she's got a lick of sense left in her head, she'll take Dallam's offer.''

"She won't," Sarboe said. "I can tell you that now. I'll tell you something else. I'm going to be busy for a day or so, but when I get back to town, you'd better be a hell of a long ways from here.''

Wheeling, Sarboe strode back to Main Street, as angry as he had ever been in his life. Rita, he thought, had known what Barrett would say. Perhaps she had even known that Barrett had sold out to Dallam. That was likely the reason she had considered Dallam's offer, why she had refused to ask Barrett for help. She was beaten. Meacham had no money. Neither did Purvane nor Sarboe. Probably Doc Zachary and Abe Tottle and Lou Fain would go along with Barrett if they knew the shape Rita was in.

He reached Main Street, breathing hard, his face red. He should have worked Barrett over. He should have broken his neck, knocked every tooth loose in his head.

"Ben." It was Doc Zachary standing in front of the hotel. "Have you seen Linda?"

Sarboe stopped. He said, "No."

Zachary hurried toward him. "I can't find her, Ben. She knew I had a baby coming today. She's not in her room and nobody's seen her since yesterday evening. What the hell has got into her?"

Sarboe was sick. There was no room for anger in him now. Just a sickness that crawled into his belly and left a clawing emptiness there. He knew the answer to this question before he asked, "Is her mare in the stable?"

"No, but she wouldn't go for a ride . . ."

Sarboe didn't wait to hear what Zachary had to say. He ran toward the stable, the doctor lumbering after him, and plunged through the archway, calling, "Buck, Buck, where the hell are you?"

The stableman came leisurely along the runway. "Right here, Marshal. What's biting you?"

Sarboe gripped his arm. "Where's Linda Kelly's mare?"

"That Corey feller came in last night and got her. About dusk it was. Took his own, too. Said they were taking a ride. Anything wrong?"

"Everything's wrong. Listen, Buck. You get hold of two men and put 'em on the fastest horses you've got. Send one to Prineville and tell the sheriff I'm heading south to pick up Shad Corey. I'm guessing he headed south, but I might be wrong. Have the sheriff send out some deputies and beat the brush. Corey might have gone in any direction."

"What do you want him for?"

"Murder, kidnapping, and running out on a hotel bill. Tell the sheriff he'll have Linda with him."

Zachary had come in. He shouted, "She wouldn't go with him."

"Depends on the cock and bull story he told her. Anyhow, I'm mighty damned sure she did. Buck, send the other man to Dallamville and tell Mike Kelly what happened."

Sarboe wheeled out of the stable and ran down the street toward his cabin. Zachary shouted, "Ben, let me go with you."

Sarboe turned back. "I don't need any help bringing Corey in, but Rita needs help and a lot of it. How much have you got, Doc?"

Zachary bristled. "That's a hell of a question. I just got out of medical school . . ."

"How much have you got?"

Zachary took a look at Sarboe's tight face. He said, "About a thousand dollars."

"Will you loan it to the company?"

"Sure, but I didn't think . . ."

"Doc, you've got to see Tottle and Fain. Don't go to Barrett. Find out how much you can raise. Go to Prineville and see what you can borrow. Tell 'em we'll put up the townsite and all our equipment. Savvy?"

"Yeah, but . . ."

"No buts. I'd do it myself if I didn't have to go after Corey."

"I've got a baby coming. I can't . . ."

"Women have babies without doctors. This has got to be done today."

"All right, Ben," Zachary said. "It'll be done."

Sarboe wheeled and ran on. He saw Rita in front of the hotel. He heard her call and waved and went on. He had always prided himself on his ability to face any situation realistically, but he was not doing that now. With Barrett selling out to Dallam, it was a wild and crazy hope to count on Zachary and the others, and he certainly could not expect help from Prineville, but help had to come from somewhere. It had to.

Chapter XVIII

A WOMAN'S SOUL

RITA woke with sunlight in her face. She moved toward the wall and lay motionless, eyes on the ceiling, her long amber hair spread on the pillow, shiny bright in the sunshine. She had forgotten to raise a window when she had gone to bed and now it was quite warm. She threw back the covers; she heard Curly Hewitt whistling in the room next door as he always did this time of morning. It irritated her. The wall between the two rooms might as well be made out of paper. She could hear every sound the water man made. She'd ask Abe Tottle for a room down the hall.

It was time to get up. She thought of the work that was piled up mountain high in the office, but she put it out of her mind. She sat on the edge of the bed and took off her nightgown, then she heard Curly slam the door and stomp down the hall. The man must weigh three hundred pounds, she thought. She lay back on the bed, utterly relaxed. It was the first time for weeks that she had permitted herself the luxury of idly lying here. Now for some reason she had no urge to get up.

Dallam had said twelve hours. The time was nearly gone, but it didn't make any difference. Ben Sarboe wouldn't let her take Dallam's offer. Ben was right. It was better to be licked clean and walk out with the clothes on her back than to take the crumbs George Dallam was willing to give her.

She thought with shame how close she had come to taking those crumbs. She had gone to Otis Barrett the afternoon before and, beating down her pride, had asked for a loan. He had given her a lecture about money and turned her down. In her thinking he had been her ace in the hole, but he had turned out to be the lowest card in the deck. That, she knew, was the reason she had weakened and had decided to take anything Dallam offered.

It was a strange thing, she thought, how much she and Ben had changed since she had come to the Deschutes. She had been so determined, so full of her dreams, so sure of success, and Ben had been "the old man of the mountains," satisfied with the quiet and primitive life he was living. Now they had reversed themselves. There was a stubborn strength in Ben she had not known was there; a weakness in her she had never dreamed she possessed.

She glanced at her body, the soft full curve of her breasts, her slim waist, the roundness of hips. She thought with brief bitterness of Linda Kelly, small and cuddly, Linda who had never known the hell of her thoughts and desires because she lacked a strong will of her own. She would be more than willing to let the man she loved dominate her life. That, to Rita, had always seemed a sort of sacrilege.

She rose and dressed, and hope rose in her again. Ben refused to be beaten. But broke or not, he aimed to fight, and in the thought of his strength she found strength for herself. She brushed her hair and pinned it up, gave her skirt an adjustment until it felt right on her hips; and went down the stairs. She would see Ben before she ate breakfast. She had racked her brain and she had come up with nothing that promised success, but Ben must have some plan in mind or he would not have been so sure of himself last night.

As Rita crossed the lobby she saw Ben run past the hotel toward his cabin. She hurried into the street and called, but he only waved at her and kept on. There was something in his face and the way he ran that warned her of trouble. She hesitated a moment, thoughts of a dozen terrible disasters flashing through her mind, then she ran after him. When she reached his barn she saw that he had saddled his horse.

"What is it, Ben?" Rita asked.

He backed his horse out of the stall. "Shad Corey murdered Holt Ricket. I'm going after him."

He couldn't leave. Not now. For a moment she clawed her mind for a way to hold him, but there was a hardness in his face that was not like him. Even before she opened her mouth she knew that no power on this earth could make him stay here.

"You can't bring Holt back to life by fetching Corey in. He'll kill you, Ben. He'll dry gulch you." She stopped, for she sensed that she was going at this wrong. "Ben, have you got any proof Corey did it?"

"Enough. When I get him in the jug, I'll get the proof out of him." He faced her, the reins in his hands, and added, "That ain't all. He's got Linda."

So that was it, she thought bitterly. Linda was more important to him than the success of their project, than beating Dallam. Linda was more important than anyone else and suddenly she was furious.

"You're a fool, Ben," Rita cried. "If Linda's with him, it's because she wants to be."

"You know better than that. I don't know how he worked it, but you know damned well she couldn't ride off with a man like Corey."

"I don't know anything of the kind. She danced with him on the Fourth, didn't she? He's been seeing her. She's man crazy, Ben. Let them go."

"No. She's decent, Rita."

"Decent?" Rita laughed bitterly. "Well, I won't say she isn't, but think of me, will you? Think of what we have here. If we've got any chance of winning, it's you who will have to win for us. You know that Dallam was terribly sure of what he could do or he wouldn't have come here last night."

"I've thought of that," Sarboe said tonelessly. "Verd probably has something up his sleeve, so you'd best get some Winchesters to Purvane. Tell him to fight and I'll get back as soon as I can."

"Fight! Ben, think about what you're saying. You're the one to fight. Fred told you that the first night he was here. Suppose Verd blows up our flume? Or runs our men off the job? Or smashes up our equipment? We're finished. Of all the times to run out . . ."

She stopped. He was angry, so angry that she thought for a moment he was going to strike her. But he made no motion. He just stood there, looking at her in that hard, tough way. Then he said, "Remember it was your idea for me to pack this star. It comes first. It has to come first to any man who pins it on if he's worth a damn."

She gripped his arms. "You're not fooling me, Ben. You're in love with Linda. You're going after them because you don't want Corey to have her."

"No," he said. "I'm not in love with Linda. I'm in love with you which probably doesn't mean a thing to you. When you showed up here, I thought everything was going to be all right, but I was wrong. You'd changed. Maybe I had, too, but it was mostly you.''

He pulled away from her and stepped into the saddle. She cried wildly, ''If you love me, Ben, you won't leave now. If you ever loved me, you'll stay here where you're needed.''

He shook his head, looking down at her, the morning sun falling sharply upon his face. His gray eyes were somber, his square jaw set. He said, ''I'm going where I'm needed, but don't ever doubt that I love you. If I don't come back, remember that. If I do come back, remember it if it makes any difference to you.'' He took a long breath. ''But I reckon it don't. You've got to make everybody think your way and do your way and that don't go with me.''

He reined around and touched his horse up and presently he was lost to sight in the pines. She turned toward town and she was crying. *If it makes any difference to you.* He was such a fool. He should be able to see how much difference it made.

She wiped her eyes with her handkerchief. She could not let anyone see her cry. Not Rita Gentry. Then quite suddenly, she remembered Linda's saying, ''You've still got a woman's heart. In the end you'll listen to it.'' She was listening now as she had never listened to it before.

She wanted Ben Sarboe more than all these things she had thought she wanted. A town. An irrigation project. Prestige and wealth. This other thing which she had valued so highly, this wanting to make a place for herself in a man's world. She had said that many times, she had thought it more times than she had said it, but now, with stark clarity, she saw herself as she appeared to Ben Sarboe, and it was not pretty. ''You've got to make everybody think your way and do your way.'' It was true. She had shaped Fred Purvane and most of the others, all but Otis Barrett who placed money above everything else.

She stopped and wiped her eyes again. Bill Packard was standing in front of the townsite office, waiting for her. She walked on toward him, her head high, her face masked against the pressure of the emotion that was in her. She had told herself weeks ago that Ben Sarboe was out of her reach, so she had tried to make other things compensate for that loss. They never would.

Now Ben had said he loved her. She didn't know why he did. She didn't want to know why. It was enough to know that he did. If he came back she would remember it just as he had told her to; she would show him how much difference it did make. She would show him if it meant getting down on her hands and knees.

She came to the townsite office and Packard touched his hat to her. He said, "Morning, Miss Gentry."

"Good morning, Mr. Packard." She gave him a quick smile, wondering if he could see the turmoil that was in her. She unlocked the door, saying, "Come in."

He followed her, shaking his head when she motioned to a chair. "I'll stand, ma'am. I know you're busy and so am I, but I just wanted to tell you that this country looks awfully good to me. You and Sarboe and Purvane look good to me, too. I guess that's the reason I believe in the country. You've got to believe in the people who are doing something or you can't believe in what they're doing."

"Thank you," she said, wondering what he was getting at.

"Well, Purvane has been stewing about some of the cuts he's made through the lava, and when he ran water into the ditch, it just trickled away. Well, sir, I seen a trick worked up in Eastern Washington, so I told him about it. You fetch in some clay and put it in the ditch, then you get some sheep and you drive 'em back and forth. All them little cracks get sealed up. Purvane didn't take no stock in it, but I got him to try it." Packard grinned with boyish pride. "It sure worked and Purvane had to eat a little humble pie. You'll have water on most of the segregation by fall as sure as I'm a foot high."

"We're beholden, Mr. Packard," Rita said wearily, "but you might as well know how it is. I'm broke. Dallam came in last night and offered to buy us out at twenty-five cents on the dollar."

Packard had his hat in his hand and was turning it, gripping the brim tightly with his big fingers. "I made up my mind that Dallam was a crook. He tried to get me to settle on his segregation, but I'd been watching that two-bit ditch his crew was digging. I reckon he was just working at it to keep the state engineer off his neck. He ain't spending no more'n he has to. Why, that ditch won't carry half enough water for the acreage he's got and yours will."

"We've tried to do an honest job," Rita said, "but honesty isn't enough. We're licked."

"No you ain't," Packard said quickly. "I remember I talked downright ornery the first time I came in here. I've always been suspicious of anyone who had money. That's why I said the things I did, but then later I seen you and Sarboe was on the level and you wanted to help the country and the people." He cleared his throat. "I'd heard some talk about your being hard up. That's why I'm here. Ma'am, I'd like to loan you what little I've got."

Her mouth went dry. She stared at the big man, wondering if he had more than fifty dollars. "Thank you, Mr. Packard," she said, "but you don't have much idea how money melts on a project like this."

"I think I do, ma'am. I've got two thousand dollars I can spare. It's in a bank in The Dalles, but I'll send for it right away. I done something else, too. I had some neighbors where I lived who want to try it on irrigated land. We did think some of going to the Yakima country, but land is mighty high up there, seventy-five dollars an acre or so. Won't be more'n ten or twelve here I judge. Well, I sent for them to come down. There'll be 'bout twenty families and they'll be along in a month or so. They've got a little money. They ain't the riffraff that comes looking for something for nothing." He cleared his throat. "You hang on till they get here and you'll make it all right."

Rita leaned forward, lips lightly pressed, eyes fixed on his wide, sunburned face. "Why are you doing this, Mr. Packard?"

He shifted his weight uneasily. "Well, like I said, I believe in the country and I believe in you folks." He looked down at the toes of his cowhide boots. "And then I'm sorry about what I said that time. I'd got so I didn't trust nobody. Then I seen how Sarboe fought and I've watched you spend money like it was water. Well, dog-gone it, ma'am, I'd just like to help out a little."

She smiled at him. "Mr. Packard, we'll hang and rattle. If you can get twenty families here by the first of September who'll take eighty acres apiece, we'll make out."

"They'll be here, ma'am. That's a promise. Fact is, I was kind of scouting for 'em. They'll come on my say-so."

Outside a rider brought his horse into the street on a dead run, calling, "Sarboe! Sarboe!"

Rita ran outside. The man reined up in the street, dust clouding him. She said, "Sarboe isn't here."

She saw then that he was one of Purvane's straw bosses. He wiped a hand across his dirt-smudged face. "That's sure a hell of a note, miss. We need him bad. I was heading for Prineville to get some more lumber when I spotted a band of riders. Twenty or more, looked like. They was headed for the ditch. I was a long ways from 'em, but looked like Verd Ricket was leading 'em."

She stood motionless, her mind gripping this. It was what Dallam had meant by his threat. Things would happen, he'd said. If she didn't take his offer, she'd wind up with nothing. Packard's two thousand wouldn't help if the flume was blown up, the big tent burned, their equipment destroyed. She ran toward Abe Tottle's store, bitterly condemning herself because she had not started the Winchesters toward camp as Ben had told her to.

Chapter XIX

PURSUIT

SARBOE rode south, trying to keep his mind on Shad Corey, trying to outguess him, and failing. He had supposed Corey would make a run for it, that he would put every mile he could between him and Swift River as quickly as possible, but he was wrong or Corey would not have taken Linda with him. Obviously a man could not make his best speed when he had a woman with him, even a strong woman who wanted to go. Linda was not strong and she was not a particularly good rider, and Sarboe was very sure she wouldn't want to go along.

He passed the spot where Curly Hewitt had found Holt's body, the sun climbing higher into a clear sky so that occasional patches of sunlight lay upon the road between the shadows of the big pines. Sarboe was not sure he was on the right track; he tried to hold his mind on Corey as he watched for some evidence that Corey and Linda had gone this way, but he could not put Rita out of his thoughts and he could not forget her words, "If you ever loved me, you'll stay here where you're needed."

Memories crowded into his mind, of the days in Cripple Creek, of the drifting years when he had earned his reputation as a lawman and the habits of a lawman had fastened themselves upon him, of his settling here on the Deschutes, satisfied for a time with the loneliness and the peace of the wilderness. Then he thought of Rita's coming, of that first evening they had spent in his cabin, and her kiss which she had said was to seal their bargain. And just before that she'd said, "You're to forget I'm a woman."

It was illogical and crazy, for no man who worked with Rita could forget she was a woman. She surely knew that. He saw now what his own course must be. First there were some pieces of unsettled business. Shad Corey. Then Verd Ricket and George Dallam. And the money that somehow must be raised to bridge the gap of time before the settlers began coming in great enough numbers to keep the company solvent. Those were obligations that faced him, then he would ride out.

Ride out! He shook his head. He didn't want to go, and that was strange because he had ridden out of many places since he had left Cripple Creek without the slightest pang of regret. But when he left the Deschutes he would be leaving the things he wanted. He had been wrong when he had been so rebellious about the change that he knew would come to this country, for any change that made a place for people to live was good. Rita had dreamed a good dream and he respected her for it, but he could not stay.

He had not intended to tell Rita he loved her, but he had, and then she had tried to use that knowledge to make him stay, to forget Linda and Shad Corey. It wasn't like her. Not the real Rita who had been so concerned about the women and the children when the May snowstorm had come, not the Rita who had planned a town where the saloons would be on one street and the stores on another.

He did not understand her. Perhaps he never would. But he couldn't stay. Not after turning his back upon the one thing that was more important to her than anything else. She would not forgive him. She had momentarily weakened enough to consider taking Dallam's offer, but he had not let her do it. Then he had walked out on her and the project.

Perhaps Rita honestly thought Linda had gone with Corey of her own free will. She had certainly thought Ben

Sarboe's first duty lay with the project. No, she could not forgive him. The disagreements they had had before had been nothing compared to this. So he would ride out because it was the only thing he could do.

It was midmorning when he came to Hod Dakin's cabin. Dakin lived here with his wife, using his fishing pole and gun and traps to wrest a living from the wilderness. When Sarboe reined up and called, Dakin opened the door and stepped out, asking, "Ain't you riding a little early, Ben?"

"Yeah, but not early enough," Sarboe answered. "Seen a man and woman ride by?"

Dakin moved toward Sarboe, frowning. He said, "That I did. They stopped last night and got a drink. Woke me and the missus up." He pulled at his ragged beard. "Anything wrong?"

"Plenty. I want the man for murdering Holt Ricket."

"Well, I'll be damned. You know, I figured something was wrong, but I didn't know. The woman stayed on her horse. The man filled their canteens and took a dipper of water out to the woman. It was too dark to get a real good look at her, but I had a notion she'd been crying."

It was the first real proof Sarboe had had that he'd guessed right. Now it struck him that it was queer Corey had stopped here to give him that proof. "Get any idea where they were headed?"

Dakin nodded. "Silver Lake. The damned fool was figgering on cutting through the lava cast forest."

"Why, he's loco. Why didn't he go on the road . . ." Sarboe stopped. This was queer, too. Probably a false clue that Corey had dropped, hoping to throw Sarboe off the track. "You tell him he was making trouble for himself?"

"I sure did, but he claimed he'd been through there before." Dakin shrugged. "Hell, it wasn't any of my business."

"Thanks, Hod," Sarboe said, and rode on.

The lava cast forest lay east of the road, a weird, desolate region covering several square miles, a broken lava desert with ravines and sheer walls twenty feet high. The region got its name from the casts that had been made two thousand years ago when molten rock had flowed in upon a pine forest. It was an ideal place for an ambush, and now, thinking about Shad Corey, Sarboe decided that was the reason Corey had left a plain trail.

Within the hour Sarboe found a woman's handkerchief in the road. Dismounting, he picked it up. The letters LK were embroidered in the corner. It was no accident, Sarboe thought, that it had been dropped here. He walked slowly, leading his horse, and presently he saw that two horses had left the road and turned directly eastward.

Sarboe could make a reasonable guess as to what was in Corey's mind. The man had his own peculiar pride. He had swallowed it when he had obeyed Sarboe's orders to keep his gun in his room and let Linda alone. On the Fourth he had flouted these orders; he had challenged Sarboe to a shooting match and had been turned down.

Mounting, Sarboe followed the tracks. It would strike Corey's perverted sense of drama, Sarboe thought, to lure him here and dry gulch him, and it would be safer than along the road where the pines gave thin cover. That was probably the reason Corey had brought Linda. He wanted Sarboe to know that he had the girl, for it was the one lure that would be certain to bring Sarboe.

The sun was noon high now, laying a brittle heat upon the dry earth. The pines were scattered here, and patches of sunlight alternated with skimpy shade from the trees. Sarboe crossed outcroppings of lava from an ancient flow. He lost the tracks, but it was not important. He did not doubt now that he would find them in the lava cast forest, so he made the best speed he could through the broken country, forcing his horse steadily up a slope that tilted at a sharp angle. Then he was out of the timber and among the lava casts.

Sarboe had been here once before with the sheriff. He pulled up, scanning the desolate country ahead of him. A high ridge lay to the east and, according to the sheriff, the molten lava had poured out of fissures along this ridge, running down its slope to spread out into what had been a stand of big pines.

Even with the knowledge that Corey was not far from him, Sarboe could not help thinking of that bygone age when this horror had rolled out upon the earth, flaming rock splashing against the pines and bringing the burning trees crashing down with a great splintering of trunks and limbs. Pitch smoke must have lifted toward a darkened sky; there would have been the thunder of exploding gases, and then the lava had cooled around the trunks of the trees, leaving the casts which had survived. Some were round, perpendicular holes twenty feet deep; others were horizontal tunnels that had been formed around trees which had fallen.

Sarboe rode on, slowly, his horse's hoofs dropping against the lava with a hollow ring, sounding as if the earth was empty below the rock crust. Then he saw two horses ahead of him. Linda's mare was one, Corey's black gelding was the other. Corey and Linda would be close. He pulled up and sat his saddle for a time, wondering. There were a dozen places, a hundred places, where Shad Corey could be hiding in the crevices and cracks of the lava, holding a gun on Sarboe while he waited for him to come closer.

If Sarboe went on, he'd be shot, but he couldn't turn back, for he knew the hell through which Linda had lived these past hours. Ben Sarboe would not be alive today if it had not been for Linda's care, but to go on and get himself killed would not do the job he had come to do.

He could swing east to the top of the ridge and look down upon Corey's hiding place, but from here it appeared that the west slope of the main ridge was too steep for a horse to climb. More than that, he did not know Corey's location and Sarboe might inadvertently come within gun range.

There was only one thing to do now and that was to wait, even though waiting would be hard on Linda. Dismounting, he hunkered beside one of the perpendicular casts, quite casually as if he were here to look at the scenery. He rolled a smoke and fired it and began tossing small chunks of lava into the cast, listening to them bounce around until they reached the bottom, but he was not as idle as he wanted to appear. Actually he was making a careful study of the broken country ahead of him.

The horses were south and to his left. A low ridge of piled-up lava lay to his right. He was convinced that Corey was waiting atop that ridge. If Sarboe rode on in the direction he had been following, he would pass within easy revolver range of anyone on the ridge.

It was an old game to Sarboe. From past experience he knew he could stand as much nerve pressure as any man, and he had a feeling that Shad Corey was neither as tough nor as experienced as he let on. Otherwise he would not have gone to the trouble to lay a trap like this, nor would he have been naive enough to believe that Sarboe would stumble blindly into it.

Sarboe finished his cigarette and rolled another, listening to a squirrel's scolding chatter. He rose and, thumbing a match to life, fired his smoke. Moving casually as if he thought there was nothing for him here, he swung into the saddle and turned his horse around.

Corey's reaction was exactly what Sarboe had hoped it would be. He jumped up, calling, "Sarboe, you too yellow to come after me?"

Sarboe swung his horse back; he dug in the steel and headed directly for the ridge. He heard Linda scream as he dropped low in the saddle. Corey's gun thundered, the slug falling short. Then Sarboe was within range and the second bullet snapped by within a foot of his head.

Corey was standing at the edge of the ridge that made a steep wall directly below his feet. He started to drop down as if suddenly realizing he made too big a target standing upright, then for some reason that was not clear to Sarboe at the moment, he straightened and let out a shrill, involuntary cry of pain. Sarboe let go with his first shot, and Corey tumbled down the slope in a wild tangle of arms and legs.

Sarboe thought he had hit the man. Close now, he pulled up and swung down, and saw he was wrong. Corey had hung onto his gun and he was on his feet, staggering forward, his face bloody from scratches that jagged points of lava had given him as he plunged down the ridge.

Corey threw a slug that came close, then Sarboe, running toward him, fired three times fast, each shot hammering into the echoes of the one before. Corey dropped his gun and fell forward in the loose-jointed way of a man who has lost all his controls at once.

The impetus of Corey's forward movement had brought him to Sarboe's feet. He lay facedown in the rough lava. Sarboe stood over him, watching, his gun lined on the man, but Corey did not move. Stooping, Sarboe turned him over and felt of his wrist. There was no flicker of pulse; his pale eyes stared up out of a barren, lifeless face.

Sarboe lifted his head to look at the ridge. Linda was standing where Corey had been a moment before. Sarboe shouted, "You all right, Linda?"

She was pale and she was trembling, but her voice was steady when she said, "I'm fine, Ben." She started down the slope. Sarboe holstered his gun and moved toward her. She slipped in her anxiety to reach him and fell. He was there then, catching her and swinging her down to the base of the ridge. She clung to him, her face against his shirt, and she began to cry.

For a long time he held her that way. Then he asked, "You're sure you're all right? Corey . . ."

"He didn't touch me," she whispered. "I was just bait to pull you into a trap so he could kill you."

She straightened and wiped a sleeve across her face. "He took my handkerchief and left it on the road. He had it all figured out. He said the only logical way for him to leave the country was to go south. You'd know that, you'd stop at Dakin's place and Dakin would tell you Corey was coming here. You'd see the horses and think we'd been thrown, and you'd come to see about it and he'd kill you." She raised her hands to his face. "Ben, I was afraid it would work like he'd planned it. I couldn't have stood it if he'd killed you. I'd have killed him, some way."

She was, he saw, almost hysterical. He said, "I'll take you up with me. We'll get your mare."

He turned her toward his horse, one arm around her, and half carried her across the rough lava. He sat her in the saddle and stepped up behind her. She leaned back, her head against his chest, slack-bodied as if strength had gone from her. She said nothing until he reined up and, swinging down, lifted her out of the saddle, and still she clung to him as if she could not realize he was safe.

"We'd better get down to the road before dark," he said. "Do you think you can ride?"

She stepped back, her eyes searching his face. She asked, "Why did you come after me?"

"I didn't figure you were with him because you wanted to be. Besides, he murdered Holt Ricket."

"You had no proof of that."

"I'd have got my proof."

"I knew Rita would say I'd run off with him. Why did you think I didn't?"

There was no use to tell her she was right about what Rita had said. Sarboe turned away, saying, "I'll get your mare." When he had led the mare to where she was standing, he said, "I told you once that Corey was no good for anybody. I figured you'd believe me whether you'd admit it or not, so I knew you hadn't run off with him."

She was still watching him as if hoping to see something in his face he had not put into words. She turned and he helped her into the saddle. Then she said, "He told me Mike had been hurt and he was taking me to him.

I believed it.'' She made a small gesture as if disappointed in herself. ''I never questioned it until after we left Dakin's place. I thought I could forget Mike was my brother, but I can't, Ben. I just can't.''

''I thought it was something like that,'' Sarboe said. ''You ride on. I'll catch up.''

By the time she reached the fringe of timber Sarboe was beside her, leading Corey's horse, the body lashed facedown across the saddle. She did not look at the dead man; she kept her eyes straight ahead. The sun was well down toward the Cascades now, shadows lengthened behind their horses, and evening coolness moved in upon them.

It was not until they came to the road and turned north that she felt like talking. She said, ''Your riding in that way was the bravest thing I ever saw.''

He laughed shortly. ''Don't get me wrong. When I got the smell of things, I thought Corey would show himself if I headed back. When I rode toward him, I judged he wouldn't be shooting very straight because he'd be jumpy. Besides, a man riding fast and down low ain't as easy to hit as you think. Corey wanted me to believe he was tough, but I had an idea he was mostly show.''

''I don't know how tough he was, but he was mean, Ben. Just plain mean. He talked a lot. Told me Holt had shot his father. He said Verd was to blame for the trouble. There was a man in New Mexico who knew where the Rickets went. The Shadwells, that was Corey's real name, finally got it out of this man where the Rickets had gone. The Shadwell boys cut cards to see who'd come after Holt, and Corey was the one who got the high card.''

''Holt was the only one he wanted?''

She nodded. ''He shot Holt in the back because that was the way Holt had shot his father. But you were the one he really hated, Ben. He hated you more than he did Holt. He said he was going to get you because you made him let me alone and made him put his gun up. He'd been in the lava cast forest before, so he figured out how he'd get you up there and ambush you and then throw your body into one of those holes and then put rocks on top of you." She shivered. "He said no one would ever find the body."

"There's one thing I don't savvy," Sarboe said thoughtfully. "I aimed to get to the bottom of that ridge. I thought I could crawl through the rocks until I spotted him or lay low until he came hunting for me, but for some fool reason he decided to jump off."

"He didn't decide that," she said with pride. "When you swung your horse around and started to ride in, I yelled. He hit me and knocked me down. He got so anxious about you that he forgot me, or maybe he thought he'd knocked me out. Anyhow, I jabbed a pin into him. It was a long pin and I shoved it as hard as I could. He was standing close to the edge and he went over without intending to."

Sarboe grinned at her. "Looks like I'm beholden to you again."

"You aren't beholden to me for anything," she cried. "You came after me. I'll never forget that. Rita didn't want you to, did she?"

"No."

"Are you going to marry her?"

"How can I?" he demanded, angered by the question. "I'm just another man to her."

"You're so terribly blind," she said softly. "Rita's mixed up about what she wants, but if you want her, you can make her see that you mean more to her than the town and the ditch and her crazy idea that she's got to show men she can do big things. She's too proud and too stubborn to come all the way to you. You've got to go to her."

"I won't crawl to her," he said hotly.

"She wouldn't love you if you did. You've got to beat her down until she'll come halfway. You don't know it, but you've beaten her down already."

"I hadn't noticed it," he said. "Why are you saying this?"

"I want you to be happy. I'd make you happy if I could, but I'm not your kind. Rita is. You two belong together. I saw that the first day I was in your cabin and you walked across the meadow with her. She had changed her mind about fishing, hadn't she?"

"Yes."

"She changed it because of me. She wouldn't admit it, but she was jealous. Why do you think she came to the Deschutes in the first place?"

"To dig a ditch," he said angrily. "She said I was to forget she was a woman."

"Oh, you are blind," Linda cried. "Do you think any woman with the pride Rita has would come out and say she was there because she loved you, that she was chasing you? I guess you know men like Shad Corey, but you don't know the first thing about women. I've thrown myself at you, but it's not enough, is it, Ben? It's just not enough."

He was silent for a time. It was strange, he thought, that here was a girl he should be able to love, who wanted him and was not ashamed to let him know it. But she was right. It wasn't enough.

He said finally, "I'm sorry, Linda. I just can't help it, being in love with Rita."

"I know," she said softly. "I know. That's why I want you to marry Rita. You'll probably think I'm crazy, but it'll give me a sort of secondhand happiness. I won't stay in Swift River. I'll be on your conscience and that's not the way I want it."

"I'll be riding along, too," he said, "as soon as things are settled."

"What things?"

He told her about Dallam's and Mike's being in Swift River, of Rita's being broke, and Dallam's threat that things would begin to happen if they didn't take his offer. She was silent for a long moment, then she said, "I had given up hope of making Mike quit Dallam, but I'll try again."

He thought of Mike's saying he was just working for Dallam now, and he remembered the bitterness that had been in the redhead's voice. He said, "It might work this time. I kind of think it will."

Darkness had settled around them now; the last trace of sunset had left the western sky. The pines pressed against the road in two tall walls; the sky was a starry ribbon overhead. Then a lamp in Hod Dakin's cabin made a pinpoint of light ahead of them.

"I'm tired, Ben," Linda said. "I'm too tired to ride into Swift River. I'll stay with the Dakins if they'll let me. Why don't you go on and do what you have to?"

He hesitated, knowing that time held the answer to everything now. Rita had been right about one thing. If Verd blew up the flume and smashed the company's machinery, the last chance of survival was gone. It might be too late now.

"Sure, Hod and his wife will keep you," Sarboe said. "If it's all right with you, maybe I'd better get along."

"Of course." She reached out and touched his hand. "Good luck, Ben."

"I'll be needing that luck," he said.

Sarboe rode on and borrowed a horse from Dakin. By the time he had changed saddles and asked Dakin to bring Corey's body in the next day, Linda was there and Mrs. Dakin had taken her into the cabin. He left without seeing her again. He rode fast, the night wind breathing through the pines, and he thought of Linda's saying, "You've got to go to her." But he couldn't and Rita would not come to him. He was sure of that, for he understood Rita better than Linda thought he did.

Chapter XX

Decision

IT WAS NEARLY dawn when Sarboe reached Swift River on a spent horse. As he clattered into the deserted street and turned into a stable he saw that there was a light in Doc Zachary's office. A sleepy hostler came down the runway, yawning and rubbing his eyes.

"Saddle the fastest horse you've got," Sarboe said, "and rub this animal down. Give him a double feeding of oats."

"I'll take care of him, Marshal," the man promised.

"I'll be back in a minute," Sarboe said, and wheeled into the street.

Zachary must have heard Sarboe ride into town, for he had opened his office door and stood peering into the darkness. Sarboe ran along the walk, heels pounding on the planks, then Zachary saw him and called, "Ben, that you?"

"It's me right enough," Sarboe said. "Anything happen?"

"We got the baby, double measure. Twins. Both are doing nicely and the mother . . ."

"Hell, I want to know about Rita . . ."

"Cool down, boy," Zachary said. "Rita's all right. What about Linda?"

"I left her at Dakin's place. She's just fagged out. Now if you don't tell . . ."

"Come in," Zachary said, and stepping back, sat down at his desk.

Sarboe stood in the doorway, looking at the slack-shouldered doctor and thinking that the man had aged ten years in the weeks he had been on the Deschutes. So had Rita and Purvane, and Sarboe supposed he had. He wondered momentarily if the job was worth the price they were paying and then put the question out of his mind.

"Well?" Sarboe demanded.

Zachary rubbed his face. "Here it is, Ben. Verd Ricket shot his father."

"Cap's dead?"

Zachary nodded. "Died just a little while ago."

"How did it happen?"

"Cap rode into town after you left. Fetched in some steers and wanted help to gather the rest of them off Pine Mountain, but there wasn't anybody to go with him. We'd just got word that Verd was riding toward camp with a bunch of toughs. Most of them were the men Purvane fired after you had your fight with Verd. They'd been working for Dallam, you know. Bill Packard was here. Rita got all the Winchesters and shells Abe Tottle had in the store and headed for camp. Cap and Packard went along."

Zachary rubbed his face again. "I couldn't go on account of the twins were coming. By the time Rita got to camp, Purvane had sent most of the men to town. I guess that was what Verd wanted. Anyhow, Purvane just kept the ones who came with him last April. Gave them rifles. Verd didn't start anything. He camped a little below Purvane's camp. Well, Cap couldn't wait. He went over there. Told Rita he'd promised to stop Verd and he was going to do it. Verd came out to meet him. Nobody knows what was said. They jawed awhile and Cap tried for his gun. Verd was too fast."

Sarboe stood motionless, staring at the doctor's stubble-covered face. It seemed incredible, yet he understood, for he had sensed the self-condemnation that had been in Cap Ricket for what had happened to Holt. Too, Cap had blamed Verd. He had tried to do his best for Holt and his best had not been enough. Perhaps through the years he had learned to hate his older son as much as Holt did, and in a moment of frantic rage he had tried to kill Verd, hoping that it would balance his failure with him.

"Then we haven't got a murder charge against Verd," Sarboe said.

Zachary shook his head. "It was a fair fight, but I just can't understand it. A father pulling a gun on his own son . . ."

"You would if you had Verd for a son. Any trouble since?"

"Not that I've heard. They brought Cap in and I've been here with him. Verd seems to be waiting." Zachary spread his hands. "But why, Ben? What's he waiting for?"

"Maybe he thinks he'll scare Purvane, or maybe he figures Purvane will start the ball. You never know what goes on in a head like Verd's got. Rita out there?"

"Yeah, she's there. Nobody could make her stay in town. And Ben, we've raised some money. You and Rita can hang on for a couple of months. By that time the settlers will be rolling in. Packard's got a bunch he's sure of. I talked to Abe Tottle and Lou Fain. They're throwing in five thousand apiece and Tottle's gone to Prineville. He says he knows where he can get another ten thousand."

Sarboe leaned against the door jamb, relief washing through him. He said, "I want to see Dallam's face when he hears it."

"That isn't all," Zachary went on. "Cap was conscious for a while. He gave us all the money he had, about fifteen hundred, and signed over his ranch. He said his steers were yours for the taking."

"Rita know about this?"

Zachary shook his head. "You can tell her. I told you once that all hell couldn't stop her."

"No, I guess not," Sarboe said, and left the doctor's office. Zachary would never know how close Rita had come to being stopped.

Sarboe left town on the livery horse, a brown gelding that had the speed he needed. He was remembering the time in Cripple Creek when he and Cal Gentry had ~~spected~~ a robbery and Rita had ridden out of the aspens ~~~~ the trail, a six-gun on her hip and a Winchester held across the saddle horn. In that one way Rita had not changed at all. She was out there with the picked men Purvane had kept, and she would live or die with them.

Dawn light worked across the sky and the stars died, and it was full daylight by the time Sarboe was out of the pines and among the junipers. He had angled northeast from town so that when he came into the open atop a ridge, he could look down upon Purvane's camp.

Reining up, Sarboe stared down upon almost the same scene he had looked at the morning he had fought Verd. There was the big dining tent and the smaller tents where the men slept, the idle scrapers and wagons and horses, the long line of recently moved earth and powder-splintered lava rock and uprooted junipers along the right of way. But there was a difference, not in what he saw, but an inherent difference which he sensed in the situation itself. This would be his last fight with Verd Ricket.

In the pale light of early morning, Sarboe could make out Verd's camp to the north. A number of men were idling around the fire, and for a time Sarboe wondered about it. Dallam was not one to waste money by hiring an outfit like this just to loiter around a campfire, nor was it like Verd to sit quietly through another day. He had tried to intimidate Purvane and his crew once before. This time he would do more than intimidate.

From where he sat his saddle, Sarboe had a view that a man in the bottom would not have. He should be able to guess what Verd planned to do, but the pieces of the puzzle did not make a pattern. Not until he looked south along the ditch to a dry wash that had been flumed. Here was a big trestle that had taken considerable time and money to build. Dallam was playing for time, enough time to break Rita, and if the trestle were destroyed, Dallam would have that time.

Even as it struck Sarboe that Purvane had made a tragic mistake in not placing guards at the trestle, he saw Verd and another man come into view in the bottom of the wash east of the ditch. He started down the slope, swinging south toward the trestle, and in that moment a sudden burst of firing broke out to the north.

Sarboe cracked steel to his horse, not knowing whether the firing meant an attack, or whether it was only an effort to distract Purvane and his men while Verd blew up the trestle. Either way, Purvane and his men could protect themselves. The trestle couldn't.

He rode recklessly, for this was not a time when he could save either himself or his horse. The slope was steep here, dotted by a few scraggly junipers and lava outcroppings that made treacherous footing. For a time he lost sight of Verd and the man with him, then he reached the ditch just north of the wash and swung south.

He heard a shot from the bottom of the wash; he reached the edge and slowed his horse as it plunged down the sharp pitch, and then another shot hammered out almost directly below him. Purvane had put a guard here, but only one where there should have been ten. He was out of the fight, lying motionless in the sagebrush.

Now, too late, the man who had shot the guard was aware that Sarboe had taken chips in the game. He whirled as the brown gelding slid to the bottom in a choking cloud of dust. It was the redhead who had sided with Verd the day Sarboe had had the fight with him.

Sarboe pulled his plunging horse up and threw a shot at the redhead. It missed and the man fired and wheeled and started to run. At once he seem to realize that flight was suicide. He lunged toward a boulder, shooting frantically, each bullet going wide. Sarboe was off his horse now and running toward the man, pulling trigger as he ran. His first bullet dug up dust in front of the redhead, the second caught him just above the ear.

It was a matter of time now, a fragment of a minute, for Verd and the man with him were on the other side of the wash. Verd was stooping, intent on unwrapping a package he had brought, the other was crouching beside him, gun in his hand, eyes searching the tall sage that covered the bottom of the wash and at the moment hid Sarboe from the man's probing gaze.

There were only two loads in Sarboe's gun and no time to shove new shells into the cylinder. He plunged through the sage just as Verd struck a match and held it to a fuse; he squeezed off a shot before the fuse caught that sliced a button from the front of Verd's shirt. Verd came upright, an involuntary motion that cost him his life. For an instant he made a wide target, and in that same instant the man beside Verd spotted Sarboe and fired, the slug whipping through the crown of Sarboe's hat.

There was the one load in Sarboe's gun and he gave it to Verd in the chest; he saw the wide, ugly face go blank as Verd went down, clawing at his shirt front. Someone else was in the fight now. A Winchester was cracking from the north side of the wash, bullets slicing through the sage and kicking up dust in front of Sarboe.

Sarboe had a brief moment of panic as the man crouching beside Verd's body threw down on him for another shot; he lunged frantically for the cover of a nest of boulders to his right, not knowing whether it was some of Dallam's men or some of Purvane's who had bought into the fight. Then the man in front of him let go with his shot. Something exploded in Sarboe's head and he sprawled facedown in the sand, hands thrown out in front of him, and he lay still, his head inches from the cover he had failed to gain.

Afterwards Sarboe had some hazy recollections of lying in his bunk and trying to sit up, of Rita's pushing him back and talking in a low, soothing voice, of Zachary's giving him something and saying to Rita, "I think he'll be on his feet by morning, but you never know about a head wound like this and he got a bad injury out of the fight with Verd. We'll just keep him quiet tonight and see how he is in the morning."

By morning he was all right. He was weak and dizzy when he first stood up and his head ached. But he was all right. He had to be. Too much of the unfinished business was still unfinished. He was alone in the cabin at the time, although there was a fire in the stove and coffee fragrance was strong in the room. Rita, he supposed, was somewhere around.

Sarboe poured water into the washpan and soused his face, being careful not to touch the bandage around his head. He was drying when Rita came in with an armload of wood.

"Get back in that bed," Rita cried. "Can't I even go . . ."

"I'm done with the bed," he broke in. "Sure a good thing I got that slug in the head. I might have been hurt if I'd got it somewhere else."

In spite of herself, Rita smiled as she dropped the wood into the box beside the stove. "Sometimes I wonder just how much of your head is bone," she admitted. "Anyhow, you get back into bed."

He sat down at the table, his lips set stubbornly. "I want some of that coffee. Then I'm riding."

She faced him, hands on her hips. "And just where are you riding to?"

"Dallamville."

She came to the table and sat down across from him. "It's finished, Ben. Mike Kelly shot and killed George Dallam."

His lips lost their stubborn set. He put a hand to his aching head, thinking he must be worse off than he realized. He said, "Say that over, real slow."

"I know," she said gravely. "I wouldn't have believed it myself if I hadn't seen Dallam's body. Kelly brought it in. You'll remember you'd had a man sent to Dallamville to tell Kelly about Linda. Dallam had been bragging to Kelly about what Verd was going to do to us to make us quit, and Kelly was mad. He said they'd both wind up in jail and he told Dallam he was a fool for trying to take what we'd done instead of building his own town and ditch system. When he heard about Linda he jumped to the conclusion that Dallam had hired Corey to kidnap Linda.''

"Why?"

Rita spread her hands. "I don't know. Maybe Kelly was out of his head. I do know I was wrong about him, Ben, just like I've been wrong about several things. I think he was honest in wanting to build up this country and he had pictured himself right in the middle of it. That's why he was so crazy mad at you and me and why he's been blind to Dallam's methods. Anyhow, he started back for Swift River with the man who had brought word about Linda. He said he kept thinking about Dallam and he knew you'd find Linda, so he went back.''

Rita rose and, bringing the coffeepot to the table, filled two cups and set one in front of Sarboe. She said, "I think the answer to all of this is the fact that Mike had dreamed for months about being the big duck in our little puddle, and he finally got it through his head that Dallam wasn't giving him any part of it. Well, he went back and started knocking Dallam around. Dallam tried for his gun and Mike shot him. The sheriff was here in town after our ruckus at the ditch. He took Mike's word for it and let him go. Seemed to me he sort of thought Mike should have a medal instead of being arrested.''

Sarboe asked, "Linda?"

"She left the country with Mike yesterday. They were going over the Santiam Pass to the Willamette Valley." Rita lifted an envelope from an apron pocket and handed it to Sarboe. "She asked me to give you this."

He took the envelope, seeing that his name was on the front and it was sealed. He raised his eyes to Rita and she shook her head as if sensing the question that was in his mind. "I didn't read it, Ben." He tore it open and took out the single sheet of paper.

Dear Ben,

I'm leaving with Mike. As I told you once before, I've tried to forget that he's my brother, but I can't.

I think a lot more of him now after what he did. I don't know what we'll do, but maybe he's finally grown up enough to go to work and forget his dreaming. Anyhow, we'll make out.

Marry Rita, Ben. I knew you were in love with her a long time before you told me. You've done a great deal for me and you said I had done something for you, so I guess it balances off, but I hope you'll never forget me and I'll always be thankful that I knew you. In spite of your stubbornness and your pride, you are the finest man I have ever known.

> Sincerely,
> Linda Kelly

Carefully Sarboe folded the paper and put it back into the envelope. *In spite of your stubbornness and pride!* The words hit him in the stomach like a club blow. He had no illusions about his virtues and his faults, but he had never realized that pride and stubbornness were faults which stood out above the others so noticeably that Linda would single them out.

Rita reached out and laid a hand on his. "I'm sorry, Ben. I tried to get them to stay. Doc Zachary begged Linda, and I told Mike we'd give him a job, but they wouldn't budge."

He said, "Thanks," and getting to his feet, walked to the door. He would liked to have shaken Mike's hand.

He put a shoulder against the jamb. The town seemed very quiet. At this moment even the sawmill was silent. He thought he could hear the murmur of the river. There would be time for fishing now. He looked up the street now toward the business block and he felt a burst of pride that was new to him. He had helped build this town; he could take some credit for the ditch.

"Packard saw you riding toward the trestle," Rita said. "He got the man who shot you. When the sheriff got there the rest of them didn't have any stomach for fighting after they found out Verd was dead. Abe Tottle had gone to Prineville. That's how the sheriff happened to decide he'd better ride over. He told the bunch they'd better get out of the county and stay out, and they were glad to do it.''

Without turning his head, Sarboe asked, "What about the money?''

"Everybody is helping out but Otis Barrett. We'll keep afloat until fall and then the settlers will be coming in.'' She rose and came to him. "Ben, you've had a lot to say about my damned fool pride and how I try to make folks think my way and do my way. Well, you're right and I'm wrong, and that's something I've never said before to anyone, but I'm not stupid. I've learned something out of this.''

He turned and looked at her, noticing again that she was almost as tall as he was, and thinking that in her way she was as strong. The morning sunlight brought out the color of her amber hair; her blue eyes were bright with the old eagerness that had always set her apart in his mind from other women he had met. He felt the familiar hunger for her stir in him, a hunger that would never be entirely satisfied.

"What did you learn?'' he asked.

"That I can't do it all myself,'' she answered honestly. "If I ever forget that, remind me of it.'' She smiled a little. "Otis Barrett decided this wasn't a good place for him to live, so he's leaving town, but the rest are staying. Swift River, you know, the city of promise on the Deschutes.''

Still he stood there, looking at her as he remembered Linda saying that Rita had to be made to come halfway to him, but he didn't know what to say that would bring her that distance. She knew he loved her. He had told her that. Now he wasn't sure that anything was really changed between them, so he said, slowly, as if groping for words, "I guess I'll be riding. You'll make out fine now.''

"You're riding across the Santiam Pass?''

He shook his head. "No. I'll just be riding.''

"To find another place where you can be the old man of the mountains?"

He shook his head again, smiling faintly. "You'll think this sounds funny, but I kind of like being an empire builder, now that I've had a crack at it."

"Well then," she said softly, "saddle my horse for me, Ben. I'll be riding along."

"You mean that?"

"I never meant anything more in my life. That's something else I've learned. Linda said that some day I'd listen to my heart. That's what I'm doing now. I want a home and I want children and nobody else will do for their father." She laughed. "I know they'll be as stubborn as little mules, but we'll manage them."

"Well then," he said, "I guess we'd better stay."

He took her into his arms and she clung to him, lifting her mouth for his kiss, and the old fire that had long been in him burst into a bright, tall flame. She could not get enough of his kiss; her slim body pressed against his and she let him know that her hunger for him matched the hunger that was in him for her.

Even then he was not blind to the future. His life would be neither peaceful nor quiet, but it would never fail in being interesting and that was the way he wanted it. No more hills to ride up to see what was on the other side. Their roots would go down into the sandy soil along the Deschutes and they would watch the people come.

WAYNE D. OVERHOLSER

WESTERNS

FREE!!
BOOKS BY MAIL
CATALOGUE

BOOKS BY MAIL will share with you our current bestselling books as well as hard to find specialty titles in areas that will match your interests. You will be updated on what's new in books at no cost to you. Just fill in the coupon below and discover the convenience of having books delivered to your home.

PLEASE ADD $1.00 TO COVER THE COST OF POSTAGE & HANDLING.

- -

BOOKS BY MAIL

320 Steelcase Road E.,
Markham, Ontario L3R 2M1

IN THE U.S. -
210 5th Ave., 7th Floor
New York, N.Y., 10010

Please send Books By Mail catalogue to:

Name _____
(please print)

Address _____

City _____

Prov./State _____ P.C./Zip _____

(BBM1)